Praise for The Book...

Todd's narrator tells us "I guess people fall out of worlds into new ones for various reasons." In finishing her late husband Tom's novella and framing it with her own, Judy Benson shows us how the fall from one world—as terribly painful as it can be—can open another, how grief can give us purpose and new life.

—Richard Telford, English and science teacher at
Woodstock Academy, volunteer with the
CT Audubon Society, where he helped found
the Artists in Residence program at Trail Wood,
and author of the forthcoming biography
of Edwin Way Teale.

The Book of Todd is a tender story of love, loss and forgiveness. The story within the story is about a childhood friendship. It took me back in time to one of my own. The central story—about the author and her recently deceased husband—reminds us how little we know about the life experiences that shaped those closest to us. And yet, we do know their hearts and values, and that is what draws us to each other. I was touched by the journey this novella offered—a road filled with empathy and curiosity towards understanding and acceptance.

—Maryam Elahi, president and CEO of
the Community Foundation of Eastern Connecticut—
a longtime supporter of the New London
Homeless Hospitality Center and the
New London Community Orchestra
and its Music City Strings program.

The Book of Todd

To Karen
with much gratitude,
Judy

The Book of Todd

JUDY A. BENSON AND THOMAS K. CLARK

JBenson Books

The Book of Todd
by Judy Benson and Thomas K. Clark
Copyright © 2025 Judy Benson

Published by
JBenson Books,
in cooperation with
New London Librarium
New London, CT 06340

Cover image by Mimi Heldman. Used with permission.

ISBNs:

Paperback: 979-8-3485-3973-3

Ebook: 979-8-3485-3976-4

All proceeds from sales of this book benefit the New London Homeless Hospitality Center and the New London Community Orchestra and its affiliate, Music City Strings.

This book is dedicated to the New London Community Orchestra and its Music City Strings program of free instrument lessons for New London youth, and the New London Homeless Hospitality Center–groups that help elevate southeastern Connecticut with beauty, creativity, dignity and caring.

This is a work of fiction. While much is drawn
from the real-life experiences of Tom and me,
it is not intended as a literal representation.

Judy Benson

Prelude

How This Began

For years, an unfinished painting hung in the spare bedroom where I would go to read, write, and pray. The size of a sandwich board sign, the canvas was filled with a lavish floral design, a few of the blooms in the bottom right corner remaining as only pale gray outlines. My husband Todd's Aunt Hilda, who once worked as an artist at a wallpaper company, created it late in her life. It came to Todd from his mother, when she cleaned out her big old house to move into an apartment for the elderly.

While the painting had a kind of formal charm, with crisp pink and white roses hovering in midair, seemingly frozen in time and space, it was the pale gray section that drew me in. I was in my mid-30s when I first hung it, still on the upward climb of motherhood and a journalism career, intent on making my mark on the world. Yet, I appreciated being reminded that there will never be enough time. We all leave things unfinished, and even these can be beautiful.

Nearly three decades later, I found myself with another unfinished work: Todd's novella. In the last days before he died, I promised him I would complete it. By then in my early 60s, I had let go of the striving ambition of my youth and relaxed into a more easily satisfied existence. So it was a bit of a shock to realize that I was now taking on the most important project of my life as a writer. If I had once been driven as myself, Anna Clarkson, I was now being propelled by an even greater purpose: to honor my husband's wish.

The path of writing the end of Todd's story became its own story. I tell it now, woven around his tale as it unfolded. This story within a story has two voices: Todd's in his fictional tale, and mine as I listened to, absorbed, and pondered his words. His voice on the page soothed me as it had in life and allowed me to touch his soul.

I. Reading the First Chapter

About a year ago, a week before he died, in the soft, broken speech of cancer's making, Todd asked me to finish his novella. Too weak to say much, he had managed a few brief sentences about how he wanted it to end. He breathed his last breath, with me, our daughter, his sister Janie, and a hospice care worker beside him—our hands on his hands, shoulders, and chest. I know the memory of that moment will always ache just below the surface, like a kneecap that never heals right from a break, reminding you of the injury as soon as you overdo. I waited more than a year to read his story because I needed the hole in my heart to heal sufficiently. I still feel adrift without him, but at that point I was ready to start searching for my new mooring.

I took Todd's story with me into the woods. Throughout our 38 years of marriage, we had always loved hiking in the woods, both alone and together. Amid the rocks and trees and far-off cawing of crows, we had our best conversations and our most meaningful silences, discovering something new about life by paying attention to nature and each other.

I was staying for a few days with some friends at a cabin surrounded by forest trails. There, I thought, I would feel safe to read Todd's story in the company and comfort of four insightful women. Julie was a recent widow like me. Jill, Jackie, and Rebecca knew other kinds of loss and pain.

I spent the first day at the cabin unpacking and getting acclimated. The second day, the five of us hiked together until late afternoon. Later, while the others relaxed with wine and cheese and started making dinner plans, I went upstairs to read, sitting upright on my cot with pillows from home tucked behind me.

I flipped through the beginning of the story until I found a break, five and a half pages into the manuscript. I would read that much, I told myself, then stop. I wanted to avoid reaching the point when hearing Todd's voice in his writing would overwhelm me, unleashing a wave of sobbing like the ones I had so often in the first months after he died.

Before I left home for the cabin, I printed the file from his computer. Titled *Cottage at the Cinder Path*, it was just 40 pages long, divided into two sections, "Early Years" and "Later Years." I had expected it to be longer. Once I started reading, I realized the length did not reflect the effort Todd had spent on it. He had worked on it for a few years, for a time attending a writing group on Monday nights.

While he was writing, I didn't ask many questions. I felt it was better to let him release what he wanted to say, free of my intervention or the thought that he should seek it. The only clue he offered about its contents was that it drew from his experiences volunteering at our local homeless shelter. He had done that for more than a decade, encountering people who had endured odysseys of mistakes and hardships that touched him profoundly. He was also deeply troubled by how the most vulnerable among us easily fall victim to those who pretend to care.

§　§　§

Cottage at the Cinder Path
Early Years: Chapter 1

I can still see myself pushing her off the low shed roof and her falling down and then looking up, afraid. I'd jumped down after her and sat down by her side.

"See, it's not far. Why wouldn't you jump?"

She didn't say anything, just sat there with tears welling in her dark brown eyes. The memory mortifies me years later. How could I have done that to her?

We had jumped off of, and onto, and into so many places together I somehow thought we were one person. It was as if my left foot hesitated to follow my right, so I had to nudge it along. But we were separate people, and now I had frightened her and felt a sinking in the pit of my stomach that had no name. I would find out much later that learning the name for remorse was no help either. We were only four and five at the time, but everything that came later seemed connected to that thoughtless push. So many other things came later, but there is that connection that I'd never shake.

Even then, it seemed I'd known Sarah Tainter forever because my parents and her dad worked for the Stiles family on their estate. Her dad took care of the grounds and gardens and lived in a cottage. My dad was the groom and managed the stables, and my mom worked as cook and housekeeper. Her father moved here with little Sarah after her mom died. Even then, I was aware that Mr. Tainter somehow knew Mr. Stiles from before.

Our parents were too busy to keep track of us much of the time, so we had a free-range life while it lasted, inhabiting a Neverland of trails and tractor paths on the fringes of the estates and farms surrounding our little world in Connecticut of the late 1950s. We could be like moles or foxes striding along a well-worn path one moment and then ducking behind a clump of bushes when we heard the grown-ups moving about, often on horseback and talking rapidly as they walked or trotted by.

The snippets of words were mostly unintelligible, but names sometimes popped out of the talking rattle: "Richard and Susan, you say?" We learned that the big important people traveled in groups or couples and sent ahead a wall of words so that we could be on the lookout. That is, except for the gardeners and farmers, who would generally say, "How do ye do young'uns?" without a pause when coming upon us. In this way, we navigated from place to place off the roads. One convenient path led to the back of an old field mostly filled in with trees and just across the street from the store and gas station at the corner that were run by an elderly couple.

"What'll it be today, James? A piece of the penny candy, Sarah?" Mr. Sweeney would ask as we stood in front of the counter examining hard balls with no money to exchange.

"Oh well, I guess not," he'd say, although he'd sometimes hand us each a piece anyway.

Sarah was one of those inquisitive and creative little girls we all remember. Before either of us was in school, Sarah started carrying the tiny Beatrix Potter books in her pocket. They became her most important possessions, I think, and she'd hunch over a book sitting on a rock in some hidden spot away from the houses. She'd carefully examine the pictures and writing for several moments before pronouncing the words. She'd remember some from hearing them over and over at bedtime, but not enough for a whole page, so she usually had to fill in some gaps. Her favorite page was the one that told of the farmer carefully placing the sleeping bunnies in his sack.

"One, two, three, four, five, six leetle rabbits!" she'd shout out when she came to that page in the Tale of the Flopsy Bunnies. *This bunny counting was supremely joyful, so repeating the phrase several times was a fitting preface to filling in the gaps before turning the page. As I recall her dialogue now, it's always more mature sounding than it could have been at the time. Maybe that's because she always seemed like an old soul, so my memories naturally project that into her voice.*

"And the bunnies don't wake up even when he piles them right on top of each other," she continued. "They just twitch a bit as they dream about running away from a big dog,"

I wasn't sure whether Sarah was reading or made that part up. I didn't know the difference.

As children often do, Sarah populated the gardens and woods around our world with the creatures she carried about in her pocket. A wooden door set into a high stone wall at the edge of the outer garden couldn't be merely an old door covering a niche holding rakes and shovels. Of course, this was the Cat Bells door and a hedgehog ran a laundry in there, just like in The Tale of Mrs. Tiggy-Winkle, *another of her beloved Beatrix Potter stories. Sarah would try opening the door quickly to catch the laundress at work before she could whisk herself away. I've always marveled at the similarity between the door in the children's book and the door in the wall at the back of the far garden. The garden wall had a grassy hill piled up right behind it, so the door could easily be mistaken for a passage into the hill and its interior mysteries. We certainly took it that way and were not persuaded that the back of the niche was merely dirt-caked stonework. Our small fingers explored every bump and pit on the inside, undeterred by the spiders in the corners and the damp, musty smell of the place. Surely a tidy room lay just beyond our reach if we only could find some lever or button to push. Such an idea fit in with my emerging worldview of places I hoped to live one day.*

At the time, our family lived in a servants' wing that connected to the rest of the house via a narrow winding stairway leading to the main house at each level, allowing me to go from cellar to kitchen to attic without seeing the family.

My room was a recess in the attic that had been finished off for servants with wallpaper and painted trim, creating a small living space with a door that opened onto the exposed rafters and rough wood floors of the unfinished attic. Nobody bothered me there, and I had a double layer of protection from the outside world when I went up to bed at night. I'd open the attic door at the top of the winding stairway, pushed on the old-fashioned button switch for the light bulb dangling from the rafters, slipped over the wavy wooden floorboards, and turned the knob of my bedroom door. Once inside, I was in my own domain, complete with a bed on an iron frame, a pine dresser, and an old leather chair three times my size. The cracks in the leather cushion pushed out stray bits of black horsehair, but it was a comfortable place to curl up. I had a window on the gabled end of the house that overlooked the garage and horse barn off to the side.

From my room, I could survey everything important going on. I don't know if the family knew—they must have known if they'd thought about it—that the servants' boy had the run of the attic. But there wasn't much up there; it just seemed to my young self like a realm apart.

Over time, I've maintained a fondness for rough unfinished spaces. Give me bare rafters and splintery pine floorboards and I feel quite at home. I once moved into a new house with a door leading to an unfinished room over the garage. I preferred that space to the finished family room that inevitably took its place. It was I who finished the space in my spare time. So because I had the double task of hanging the pieces of wallboard and nailing in the trim, I endured both the pain of continually hitting my thumb and the sadness of walling myself in.

Sarah and I were mostly outdoor playmates. I don't even remember going into her house, although I knew it was the gardener's cottage because that's what my folks called it. Her dad was Irish and was always a bit of a mystery to me. He was kindly but didn't say too much, and what I remember most were his gentle reminders to Sarah to stay nearby as we trotted off. He played the fiddle, and the sound sometimes reached my attic window on warm summer evenings.

Mr. Tainter had given Sarah a pennywhistle that she wore tucked into a leather pouch tied around her waist. He advised her to blow three loud whistles if she ever needed help and to stay within earshot for that reason. She didn't know how to play at that age but would take it out and cover the holes with her fingers in a random way to make a light, tuneless whistling sound. I see this now as similar to her "reading" of the Potter books. Before long, though, she grew adept at both reading and playing, and by the time we were in school she was well beyond me, even though I was a grade ahead.

Sarah was so fond of her ragged Potter books that she'd read one over and over on the rocks near our neighborhood, her blonde hair and eyes pointing down with the book open on her knees as she sat on her haunches for long stretches, in the way that small children seem to do so easily. At some point, she took a new tack and began imagining what came next after the bunnies escaped from the farmer or after Mrs. Tiggy-Winkle ran away from Lucy after delivering her packets of clean linen.

Sarah's sequel for Mrs. Tiggy-Winkle and her laundry became quite extended, perhaps because we'd seen muskrats about, which we took for hedgehogs and so had some backup for the obvious empirical evidence of the Cats Bells hillside doorway. I could say I participated in these creations, but that's likely an exaggeration. I mostly was just happy to listen and prod her with a suggestion or question. I've always been comfortable listening. Maybe I was born that way, or maybe I'm still hoping to hear Sarah's voice again.

As I remember, the Mrs. Tiggy-Winkle story got us into trouble after one of our visits to the hillside doorway. Mr. Tainter had shooed us away when he found the door ajar and Sarah and me inside with the rakes and shovels.

"What's got into your wee heads now? What a place for children! Off, off you go! Stay near the house. Hear?"

So we ran back to the pasture beside the gardener's cottage and climbed over the stone wall to sit under the big shade tree.

"I think we can't find Mrs. Tiggy-Winkle because she had to go home to her own people after living alone under the hill," said Sarah. "I think her mother called her home with a whistle only she could hear, and she had to run as fast as she could back to her own land without even saying goodbye to her friends here."

And Sarah went on with the words rolling out of her imagination. From time to time, she'd wrinkle her eyebrows deep in thought before going on.

"She found a big trouble there when she got back," she continued. "You see, her people make a kind of cloth, but they don't need it for clothes since they're hedgehogs. They hang it out on clotheslines and put jars underneath because it collects the sunlight in such a way that drops of honey drip from it. They needed her to come back and help make more cloth because the foxes have been raiding their village.

"Every time the foxes come, all the hedgehogs have to scurry into their dens. When they come out, the foxes have eaten the honey and knocked over all the pots and carried off the cloth. But the cloth needs to be made in such a fine way that only a few hedgehogs can learn to do it, so they needed Mrs.

Tiggy-Winkle to help them make more cloth or they would go hungry, you see."

"I'm not sure if all of that can happen, Sarah," I said. "If the foxes have the cloth, won't they just stop, since they can make their own honey and don't need to raid the hedgehog village anymore?"

Sarah widened her eyes and looked up.

"Well, don't you see, James?" she responded. "A fox won't do that. Imagine a fox hanging up a sheet and waiting for something good to come out! They don't know how it all works, you see. No, they just take off with the sheets because they think they must be important. They're probably in a heap and all covered with nasty fox stuff like shrew and mice bones and some other bits of leftover thievery. You don't know foxes at all!"

"Then Mrs. Tiggy-Winkle will make more cloth that just gets torn up and thrown away," I said. "How can she help them?"

"Yes, we need to find her and help, too," Sarah said.

So we left our perch under the tree and headed around the edge of the gardens and onto the old tractor path that headed up the hill. This seemed, after all, the most logical path into the realm of magical hedgehogs. We believed that world to be real in the way children want to believe, even though they know such things are not part of the world of grownups. It's like how children set aside one set of clothes for hard use and another set for dreamier days, with large pockets for collecting wild berries and seashells they might fancy along the way.

Our path soon crossed a small stream that flowed out of an old mill pond mostly covered with lily pads that time of year. To hop across, we used two large flat stones that seemed placed for just such a purpose and likely had served many children growing up on the old farmsteads around the pond. The path took up again across the stream, which was too slight a thing to bother people unless they ventured that way in mud season after the spring thaw and risked losing a shoe to the sucking black slop on the banks. On the other side, the path turned onto a rough gravel road that led to a dam and a stone spillway whose trickle flowed over into the stream.

Having gained this vantage point over the lily pads and the grassy expanse by the spillway, we delayed our quest in order to poke about this well-known spot and inspect this day's selection of turtles and dragonflies. Just out of reach, a bullfrog seemed to study us as his eyes glowed yellow against the murky water. He appeared to weigh the risk of the two slight interlopers and then was gone, his departure dimpling the flat water like a noiseless pebble dropping down from above. I studied the gray water between the lily pads until I saw the bullfrog's nose appear well out of reach near one of the many moss-covered logs slowly sinking into the muck where the grassy bank gave way to a long sweep of overhanging willows and oaks.

A cloud of dragonflies whirled about us as their doubled-up gossamer wings spun the sunlight into iridescent red and purple. Some rested on lily pads with their wings now stilled or slowly rising and falling. One hovered just in front of Sarah's nose, prompting her to hold out her hand. The dragonfly obliged by dropping down on her outstretched wrist. Its wings seemed to breathe as they slowly moved up and down and Sarah's brown eyes sucked the glowing blue into their deep pools. She opened her mouth to say something and then stopped. Too late. Something in the new motion must have startled the dragonfly which, after all, operates in hummingbird time, and it flitted up and darted out over the lily pads.

"Oh no! Come back!" Sarah cried. "Oh, I bet she knows how to find Mrs. Tiggy-Winkle's world. If any creature can go from one world to the other, surely it's the dragonfly. They hover and flit so easily they know all the places and can go from one to the other as quick as a mouse. Quicker."

We never did get any farther along on our Tiggy-Winkle quest that day. But the mill pond was a fine place to imagine other worlds or merely to stop and gaze about. Our folks certainly knew our steps often led there and probably figured it was as good a place as any for children to stay out of mischief for long spells. As we grew older, we remained drawn to its lure. There was endless fascination in such simple wonders as watching the turtles come and go from their favorite sunning spot on a large log sticking out into the water. When we got to school age, we'd count them religiously and so keep a running mental record of the changing numbers. Why is it that nine turtles, rather than five, sitting on a log can seem like an extraordinary fact to a seven-year-old?

§   §   §

I looked up from the page and sighed. The story was fresh yet familiar, sweet and sad at the same time. Though I knew that James and Sarah were the work of Todd's imagination, I couldn't help but visualize him as that boy, the narrator, remembered inhabiting a storybook world with his playmate, Sarah. Todd seemed to be coming back to life in those pages to reveal the person he was before I knew him. Reading it was as close as I could come to spending more time with him. But, of course, there is never enough time with the ones we love.

I headed downstairs, where Julie was stirring something on the stove that smelled of rosemary and thyme. Rebecca chopped carrots, while Jackie searched for something in the refrigerator. Jill sat on the sofa, petting her dog Pal, a tenacious and lovable Irish terrier. I walked over to her.

"Do we have time for a short walk before dinner?"

"I think so. Let me check."

A few minutes later, we were on a trail with Pal, our feet crunching the fallen leaves and acorns. The late-afternoon sun pierced through the mostly open canopy on its steady arc toward the horizon.

"I just read the first part of Todd's novella," I told Jill. She knew that Todd had asked me to finish it.

"What was that like?" Jill asked.

"I don't think I have the words for it yet. Reading it felt painful and incredibly precious at the same time. I need to take some time before I pick it up again."

We walked in silence until we came to a stream. The sound of the water gurgling over the rocks drew me back to my surroundings. The autumn air smelled earthy-sweet, the ground was jeweled with gold and scarlet leaves. For a fleeting moment, I imagined Sarah and young James crouched beside that stream, poking sticks into its surface.

"We should probably head back," I said.

"Yes," Jill replied. "My stomach tells me it's time for dinner."

II: The Crows Mourn

Several weeks passed before I picked up the novella again. But it was never far from my thoughts. I fell in love with that sensitive little boy and the narrator who gave him life, in the way your teenage self might fall in love with a character in a favorite movie. He insinuates himself into your night dreams and your daydreams; you wish he were real. You would love him completely, perfectly.

Though I loved Todd long and fiercely, I did not love him perfectly. Our marriage lasted despite ups and downs, our human flaws, and my psychological turmoil, which took me many years to finally contain. But my core feeling is not one of regret. By the end, we had long since forgiven each other for the times we had caused the other pain, and we spoke aloud our gratitude. Ultimately, Todd brought out the best in me, and I in him. And now I have his tender, intimate story in my care. He trusted me with it. I wanted to find a way to finish it that honored him. I certainly would not muck with his deliberate prose or alter the essence of his meaning.

Doubts were never far from the surface, though. Can I do this? I had earned my living writing nonfiction, not fiction. To finish his book, I would need to find a way into that imaginary world he created and remain authentic to my own voice. When I said yes to this task, I didn't really know what I was getting into. I hadn't read his book yet, after all. But Todd had trusted me with it, so I will have to trust myself.

One bright Sunday afternoon, still preoccupied with the novella, I headed to a nearby forest for a hike. I followed my favorite trail through woods, across wooden bridges, over swamps and streams to an old farm road that passes a meadow enclosed by stone walls. At the top of a long, gradual hill, the road turns to the site of an old foundation, the remains of a farmhouse that burned down in the 1940s. I sat beside the foundation, examining the stonework arch in what remained of the fireplace. My ears perked up to the sound of crows cawing overhead.

Looking up, I saw six or eight crows taking turns making calls, first solo, then in duets and trios. Black figures swooped in and out of formation. I watched, transfixed. Their circling and calling continued for several minutes until, suddenly, they quieted and flew off. What could that have been?

I rose and returned to the trail, still pondering what I had just witnessed. I wandered for a brief while before deciding to start heading home. Then just off the trail, I looked down and spotted something lying in the tall grass. Moving closer, I saw it was a dead crow, lying with its beak skyward, its glossy wings outspread. Amazed, I surmised that I had just been part of a crow's funeral, a mourning ritual. I remembered that Todd often said we are more like other creatures than we usually acknowledge. In a strange way, the crows gave me comfort with their display. I felt awe that they could share grief with me and grateful to have shared my life with someone who understood.

On the walk back, my thoughts drifted back to the novella, to the characters and the setting. I was reminded of the place Todd grew up. It was a town of farms side by side with large estates and lots of woods to explore in between. Early in our marriage, we lived in a similar kind of town on the other side of Connecticut, with lots of hiking trails nearby. I recalled one trail we hiked several times that took us to an abandoned cottage, with a faded hand-written sign in the window that read, "Property of Haldone Gee. Please Keep Out." It had a steep roof that sloped into a curl at the bottom, reminding me of a tiny ski slope. Faded yellow paint covered the wood shingles. The windows were brown with years of grime. One of the doors hung open, askew on its remaining hinge. Inside, several empty beer cans lay on the floor, around a soiled mattress in the corner.

Despite its condition, the house still held a kind of charm. As I think about it these years later, I imagine it to be the cottage where Sarah lived with her father, the cottage that the boy in the story saw many times but that always remained a mystery. In dreams, I've heard, houses represent the self. Could that care-worn but still endearing yellow cottage, I wondered, be the model for Sarah's house, and by extension, her character?

I was now ready to reenter the world of the *Cottage at the Cinder Path*, to see the world through the innocent yet perceptive eyes of that boy and his beloved playmate. Part of me felt as though I was cheating on a test, reading his book from so personal a vantage point. But I knew that while Todd was like the character James in many ways, there were also important differences. For one, Todd's father was a well-off businessman, the type who would belong to the same yacht club as men like Mr. Stiles, not be employed by them. I would keep reminding myself that this was not a memoir, but a work of imagination.

§   §   §

Cottage at the Cinder Path
Early Years: Chapter 2

At some point, Sarah and I adopted a pair of old bamboo fishing poles we found in a shed and decided they allowed us to make more of a claim on the grassy bank by the mill pond dam. These poles gave us a reason to spend countless hours studying the dimpled impressions of the water bugs skating serenely past our fishing lines. We'd find our bait behind an abandoned barn, where the pitch-forked remains of used-up bedding tossed out the back door had decayed into a grass-covered mound of worm-filled dirt. I only needed to turn over a single shovelful of dirt to fill a coffee can with worms. But Sarah always caught far more fish than I. She had such luck that she could be very choosey about which fish to keep. She'd only accept the largest sunfish or perch that landed on her hook. And very often she'd end up throwing back the same undersized sunny over and over until she got annoyed with the fish and lectured it on survival skills.

"How many times will you get all bloody and stuck by my hook?" she'd ask. "You need to learn to stay away. Now shoo!"

Between venturing out on Sarah-inspired quests and frequent trips to the fishing pond, we gradually came into possession of a worldview centered on hedgehogs, turtles, ponds, footpaths, and old dirt roads rambling off to abandoned fields that were reverting to forest. Our realm was bordered by a highway we'd been warned to stay clear of and the road by the general store. We had ventured close enough to the highway to hear the woosh of passing cars, and that certainly didn't seem a direction worth investigating any closer. There weren't other children our age around during those early years, so we had plenty of practice finding ways to amuse ourselves, especially before we were school aged. We only had two regular contacts outside our folks and the world at the Stiles estate: the owners of the general store and an elderly man who used the old mill house by the dam as a fishing cabin.

Mr. Miner discovered us fishing near the dam one afternoon and invited us to set up wherever we liked near the pond. We'd been doing that already, since property lines hadn't yet entered our minds, but were nevertheless glad for the ratification of our welcome. We'd stayed at a distance from his cabin during our wanderings and fishing and so had not yet discovered the pond's prehistoric denizens. One day, Mr. Miner invited us onto his screen porch, where we were confronted by a row of massive turtle shells leaning against the wall.

"What are these?" I asked of the shells, which were about two to three feet long.

"Oh, don't you know these are snapping turtle shells, James," he replied. "I've taken them from the pond over the years. Massive, aren't they? I reckon some are close to a hundred years old. They mostly haul out on the island over by the far end—you can see the muddy slides where they

come in and out—so I shoot them to keep the fish in the pond."

"They eat fish?!" I'd never thought about what turtles ate but never would have imagined fish to be part of their diet.

"Yes, and other things: frogs, snakes, ducks. Mainly the ducklings, since the full-grown ducks are a bit large for them."

I couldn't help but think of the monster snappers lurking underwater and grabbing the small webbed foot of a duckling and dragging it under.

"They are the top predators in the pond and live on all the other creatures," said Mr. Miner, introducing me to a new word that I would then always associate with snapping turtles and their unseen menace lurking in the depths.

"What about hedgehogs?" Sarah asked, still engaged in her Beatrix Potter story.

"Well, I suppose so," mused Mr. Miner. "Well now, I'm not sure. Do we have hedgehogs here 'bouts? Why hedgehogs?" he asked as if to himself. "Well, I expect they're safe as a rule if they are about. But I can't think as I've seen a hedgehog."

Mr. Miner suddenly recollected the two children staring up at him as if we had momentarily disappeared.

"Oh, but don't you worry," he said, again pointing to his collection. "These old shells won't do you any harm. Even if they were alive, they'd want to run from you as quick as can *be. They don't generally bother with people unless cornered. I wouldn't worry a lick about any old turtle, snapping turtle or no."*

Mr. Miner's snappers did insert a need for caution into our worldview, however, and we left the front porch stepping cautiously near the pond.

"Did he get them all?" I wondered. "He didn't say, did he? Do you think there are any more of those enormous turtles?"

But Sarah didn't answer. She took out her whistle and blew slowly, making a low sound as her small fingers tried to cover the holes.

"But we can go and see," I said. "He told us they make a muddy slide out on the island at the end of the pond. Maybe we can see the slides from shore."

"Oh, what's the difference?" Sarah said. "They're just some nasty old turtles. You go; I don't care."

We walked along in silence. The monstrous shells of the snappers crowded everything else out of my head. I thought of them sliding down into the pond, lurking in the deep, buried in the mud, snapping fish out of the water, dragging down ducklings. I couldn't let them go. Were the turtles sitting on the logs small snappers, too? Now I didn't know.

We ended up back in the basement area of the Stiles house, which had the laundry, workshop, furnaces, and passages that led to old storage bins still holding piles of coal left over from another era. We entered through the workshop side of the basement. A double door led us into the familiar area where the smell of wood shavings mixed with the musty basement odor. My dad greeted us and stopped his work on a wooden lathe, which was covered in wood shavings from one of the chair parts he always seemed to be making.

"Was wondering where you had got off to, and here's Sarah too," he said. "Her dad was over here lookin' fer her a bit ago. Better you go up an' let your mom know you're about, son. And you better head off and catch up with your dad, Sarah. Tell him dinner's at seven."

I could see Sarah's small cottage across the backyard from the wide doorway where we were still standing. It was one of the four buildings in the cluster of the Stiles' estate: the main house, horse barn, garage and gardener's cottage.

I headed up the meandering stairway that led upwards toward the kitchen and the living area. A side room off the kitchen served as a servants' work area and gathering spot. It was furnished with a dumbwaiter from the basement, worktables, a TV set, and an old upright piano. I found my mother there gathering some linen for the table while the Stiles' daughter Laurie lay splayed out on a couch with one foot on the floor.

"There you are, James," my mom said. "Why are you and Sarah always disappearing?" She didn't wait for an answer because it was an everyday question. "Laurie will be with us

for dinner tonight. Did you let Mr. Tainter know dinner's at 7?"

Head back, Laurie was staring at the ceiling. She held a hand out, with her fingers slightly spread as if she were holding a cigarette. I knew by that time that she did smoke. It was an open secret that her parents managed to ignore as long as she was discreet.

"What will they bring back this time? Will it be a necklace, a T-shirt, another hat?" she asked the ceiling.

The Stiles took a lot of trips, often for a week or two. Sometimes they'd stay in their New York apartment for a few days at a time. They had a staff to run the house and look after Laurie. A car whisked her away to school in the morning and dropped her back home.

"Or maybe it will be something really lame like the box of pink sand they brought back from Bermuda, thinking it would be just the thing for the top of my dressing table. My own little pink beachhead.

"Where's the other little beetle, James?" Laurie asked me after mom disappeared into the kitchen, "Aren't you two joined at the hip or something?"

"We are not!" I shot out, raising my voice.

"That's it? That's all you can say: 'We are not?' Or maybe you're really the same beetle that just splits up from time to time—one beetle with eight appendages. The two halves split

up at night and then zip themselves together again for another day mucking about in the dung. Dung beetles! That's it. A dung beetle pushing a clod of dung about all day. That's what you two do."

"What do you mean?"

But Laurie ignored me, of course, and went back to studying the ceiling.

"Well, let me see then," she said finally. "Come over here."

So I went over to stand by the couch, and she put her hand out toward my head.

"Hmm..., too soft for a dung beetle," she said as she stroked my close-cropped hair back and forth with her eyes shut. "Maybe some other creature then. A very fuzzy one. OK, maybe something cuter than a beetle. A badger or an otter."

So I knew she was just being Laurie, and somehow it was OK.

We'd see Laurie on and off in the day room until she was old enough to drive ... or had friends who drove. Then her visits to the servants' quarters—our end of the house—became less frequent. She always wore light blouses and skirts that billowed as she walked, giving her an air of constant motion. Her hair filled the space around her blue eyes with an unruly blonde cloud that defied control. She was the most frequent contact I had with the family. Mrs. Stiles would sometimes come into the kitchen briefly to give my mother instructions:

"We'll need a juicy steak Friday," or "William would like a big spread of seafood this weekend with raw oysters, some fish just off the boat."

§   §   §

A gap on the page followed, so I set the book down for a while. This story set on the Stiles estate was far removed from the world of homeless shelters and the people who inhabit them that I thought Todd meant to explore. Perhaps that would come later.

At this point, Todd's words stirred a longing in me to visit Stoneham, the town where Todd grew up and surely the setting of this tale. What could I find there that might be relevant? Somehow, I knew there would be something that would help me better understand his story and allow my ending to be as true as it could be. I also thought a visit there would help me as I stumbled along in this strange new territory of grief and widowhood.

What I felt most acutely at this stage in the grieving process was that my identity and sense of meaning had gone missing. I loved being Todd's wife and the mother of our daughter. She had grown up and left home, and I drew my purpose from caring for Todd with meals and companionship, encouraging him and showing pride in his work with the homeless, providing financial stability through my 9-to-5 newspaper job, which enabled him to pursue creative work as a luthier and builder of wooden boats. What would be my purpose now that I was on my own?

Todd offered me a bridge into my new life when he turned his manuscript over to me. For the time being, my identity and purpose were wrapped up in finishing his novella. Maybe that task would take me where I need to go. My faith told me this would be so. Todd and I did not always agree on spiritual matters—my faith tended toward open-minded Christianity while he was drawn to Emersonian transcendentalism. But we shared a mutual awareness of the divine presence that reveals itself throughout life, even in illness and in death. We both relied on our faith to carry us through, and I knew mine would continue to sustain me.

I thought back to unexplainable grace moments that happened during the time of Todd's illness. One night I woke from a fitful sleep on the couch in the spare room and sensed my father there, bending over to cover me with a blanket and saying, "It's going to be all right." My father had died thirty years earlier. He was a troubled person, full of unresolved pain. But in that moment, I sensed he was at peace, and that he was conveying that peace to me. About a week later I received an unexpected package in the mail from a childhood friend, containing a soft blanket. I cried tears of gratitude and disbelief as I shared my dream with Todd. As we hugged, he cried with me.

Then there was Todd's dream, which he told me about in the examining room after the doctor told us the time had come for hospice care and then left us alone. Through our tears and shock, Todd told me that soon after his initial diagnosis, he had seen Christ in a dream stretching out his arms to him and knew this moment was just ahead. He hadn't told me about it earlier. By that time his spirituality had room for both Christianity and transcendentalism—both could be true even if not literally so.

"I didn't want to scare you," he said. "But since then, I've felt the love of Christ coming closer and closer."

He repeated that phrase often on his deathbed to anyone who happened to be there. Perhaps these visions are the mind's way of coping. Do we invent them in order to find peace? I've come to think that these moments are sudden cloudbursts from God, because I need to have faith. Either way, they are precious and rare, and I am grateful for them.

III: Preparing

Over the next couple of days, I started planning my trip to Stoneham. I made an appointment with the town's historical society to see archived photos from the 1950s and 60s, when Todd was growing up there.

I decided to read two more chapters of Todd's novella before my trip and so returned to his fictional tales of a rural childhood.

§   §   §

Cottage at the Cinder Path

Early Years: Chapter 3

Mr. Stiles usually swept in and out of the house with a wave of his hand if I happened upon him. But at times, I would see him linger just outside the double door to the stable, where he'd wait in his hunting dress for my dad to lead out his gray gelding, Temping Fox. I remember details about his dress because my dad had me polish Mr. Stiles' riding boots, so I felt in some way accountable. He'd habitually tap-tap-tap his riding crop against the side of his left boot, chafing away at the fresh polish on the wide black band atop the stiff brown leather. By evening, I'd have my arm back inside the high boot, rubbing black polish into the cuff to make it like new again. I knew the boots swallowed his jodhpurs cleanly without bunching them around the cuffs because loops under each foot held the bottoms of the pant legs taut.

Mr. Stiles would pace as he waited for his horse, walking a few steps and then leaning back to spin around on his heel. The persistent pacing seemed to stretch the moment out beyond its real time, which was brief, but he never let his voice betray any hint of irritation. Before long, I'd hear Foxy coming, skittering sideways over the wooden floorboards with an uneven clatter. My dad would hold the halter as Foxy tossed his head and emerged through the wide double doors of the barn entrance. Once outside, dad held each side of the halter to back Foxy into his mounting stance.

One day I heard Mr. Stiles tell my father, "No, not yet. Let me have a look at those tender hooves first."

My dad pulled Foxy forward a bit and dropped the reins onto the ground, letting the horse know he was expected to stand still. He stood next to Foxy and, in one motion, pushed his shoulder into the horse's side, while lifting the front hoof. Horse and man then found a new balance leaning into each other. The hoof appeared as an inverted gray clod rimmed by the iron band burnished bright by pavement friction. My father's cupped hand held the hoof with the natural ease of long practice, as effortlessly as a saucer supporting a teacup.

With his free hand, he pointed to the rubber pad covering the tender flesh inside the hoof.

"The farrier's coming by on Tuesday to change the pads and apply a new treatment. We'll see how it looks then," my dad said.

"Blast! How much longer do the pads stay in?" said Mr. Stiles, not really expecting an answer. "I won't be taking any gates any time soon. What's the good of a champion horse that's half lame?"

"Well, he might'n have to be put off riding for a spell," my dad said.

"Christ almighty. Well, I've seen enough. Let's get on with it. I'm riding today anyway and then we'll see."

My dad leaned away from Foxy and dropped the hoof so he could get Mr. Stiles mounted. He bent over and held his cupped hands for Mr. Stiles' boot and straightened up as Mr. Stiles swung his leg over and took his seat. Foxy pranced sideways and bobbed his head up and down, taking on the new weight. Then Stiles was off, flexing his will with a jab of his blunt spur and the snap of his whip.

I felt a shaking in my middle. Foxy was so big I must have been just a speck to him, and yet whenever I'd walk up to his stall, he'd lower his head way down to my level and gently rub his forehead against my side. Well, I knew it was gentle even though I had to hold onto his halter and brace my feet to keep myself from being knocked over. I felt as if he was trying to rub something into me, but I couldn't figure out what it was.

I probably didn't see Mr. Stiles for weeks after that day. He'd come out to the barn without much of a warning, in fits and starts. For long stretches, I'd see him near the barn as a mere flash when he rushed up and down the drive in his long car. I came to know that his presence hovered over the barn even when he was gone for long stretches. Carpenters arrived one day to tear apart one side of the structure, setting up new stalls and removing a storage area. Some weeks later, a horse trailer pulled in with a roan gelding that my dad led into a new stall that still smelled of the fresh pine boards lining its sides. On another day, after coming in from the woods, Sarah and I discovered that Foxy had disappeared.

"Did Mr. Stiles sell Foxy?" I asked my dad. "Who bought him?"

"Now just let that be, James," my father said. "Foxy's in a good place. That's all there is to know."

"Can we go see him?"

He looked up and studied the hay bales in the overhead loft for so long I thought he'd forgotten about my question.

"Could we go see him?"

He looked down at the wide floorboards and answered so slowly that I knew not to ask any more questions.

"He's ... just ... not ... around here. Off ...off with you, now."

Early Years: Chapter 4

Along with Laurie, Mr. Miner became our primary contact with the outside world in those few years before school started, first for me and then for Sarah.

Mr. Miner taught me most of what I know about fishing. He showed us pictures of the fish in the pond, so we had an idea of the look of large-mouth bass, pickerel, sunfish, perch, and catfish. Up until our acquaintance with Mr. Miner, our knowledge of fish was limited.

"Oh, you have a sunfish," or "Oh, a perch this time," Mr. Miner would say as I held up my catch.

Up until then, we'd been simply dangling a worm with a lead weight into the water. But Mr. Miner examined our rig and decided we needed a few simple modifications. He showed us how to attach a bobber and leader and in this way upgraded our tackle.

One constant during those years became the evolving whistle-song traipsing along beside me on wanderings across the fields and through the woods. The pennywhistle Sarah's dad had given her spent less and less time in its leather pouch as Sarah moved from random twittering to the actual tunes her dad taught her. Her whistle soon became a mimic of her own high, chattering voice. She'd discovered there were myriad ways to get out an "olly-olly in-is-free," especially with pennywhistle at hand. The oll-ie could be made into a low sing-song in so many ways. The quick "in-is" could vary endlessly as the lead into the joyous "freeee," with a repeated two-pip whistle entrance just for the fun of it. Do-re, do-re, do-re ... mee-ee-ee. And then the mimic of her voice: In-is, in-is, in-is ... free-ee-ee.

So my inner ear will always hear "Ollie, Ollie ... in-is free-ee-ee" as Sarah's whistle tune. I have no memory of actually playing hide-and-go-seek at all, which was the point of the song. Surely, we spent hours and hours at it, yet the game itself is a blank for me now. What lingers are Sarah's songs and our various escapades looking for imaginary creatures in the woods. No matter where I catch a hint of the phrase, near a playground or across a backyard lawn, I hear her high whistle sailing over the ponds and fields.

One afternoon, Sarah stopped fishing after unhooking a small, bloodied pumpkinseed, the creature we preferred to call a sunfish.

"You go back home now and leave my worms alone," she said for the umpteenth time. "You're much too small to play around here." Then she placed her bamboo pole against the post-and-rail fence that trailed down to the water's edge.

As I continued to fish—the small pumpkinseeds never seemed to bother my worms as much as they did Sarah's—she lay down on her side and rested her head on her left hand. A dragonfly buzzed by and halted inches from Sarah's nose, seemingly intent on finding a landing spot there. She stuck out her finger.

"Here you go. You can hop on here if you like," she said. "What a pretty little dragonfly. Won't you come home with me and stay on my windowsill? You can come and go as you please."

When I looked over toward her a bit later, she had dozed off with her head on her curled arm, the shower of her blonde hair covering her face.

I went back to fishing and for once had decent luck. I swung in a largemouth bass keeper and two medium perches. I carefully worked the hooks out of their mouths and let them back into the murky pond water.

After a while I'd had enough of fishing and looked over at Sarah. She was still asleep, so I touched her arm and she awoke with a start.

"Oh no! Why, it was just a dream after all! I do want to be back there. Do let me go back," she said.

"But why?"

Seemingly mesmerized by her own imagination, she fell into one of her stream-of-consciousness tales. Once again, as I try to recall her words now, I hear her speaking in the voice of someone much older than she was then. Maybe Sarah always seemed someone in touch with wisdom beyond her years.

"There was this beautiful blue dragonfly that landed on my finger before I dozed off and came back for me," Sarah began. "The dragonfly picked me up and took me away with him, letting me ride between his wings. It was ever so much fun, but scary until I got used to it and didn't slip sideways or fall off. We buzzed away so fast and were way up above the pond looking down. You looked like a bit of a boy holding a stick from way up there," she said.

"Oh, you're always making up stories. It's just another of your stories."

"We were gone so long and so many things happened," she continued, undeterred. "Even though I could tell where we were, it was like seeing everything through a screen filled with tiny bright shapes, like triangles or diamonds. The grass had these tiny bits of the brightest yellow mixed in with bits of the greenest green I've ever seen. Even our muddy pond water had drops of red and green and yellow, and they moved about with a throbbing motion, red rising with a burst and green swallowing that up and then yellow pulsing through. And then the tiniest moving things caught the bits of color so they all swirled in a line, forming a long trail. Every waterbug and mosquito in the air inched along, leading an army of swirling color following behind on the water. Every now and then, we'd dart sideways and pick off a bug as if it were standing still.

"But then we followed the stream down as it tumbled over rocks, ever so close to the foam so I could feel the cool wetness on my face. Then we bobbed up again to hover for an instant under the canopy of trees with the water rushing by below in a white blur. The stream opened into a wide lake that I don't remember seeing before. Instead of the lily pads and calm pond water, we came to a wider water rippling in the wind. The dragonfly tipped into the wind and forged ahead, weaving side to side and it zipped along just inches from the water. We finally came close to shore and then we veered away at the last second as a large bullfrog sprang at us, a blizzard of green and yellow swooping by within an eyelash of me and my mount. Then we were past and the swirling blizzard sank back into the water, swallowed up by a siege of purple diamonds that sank into a pool of midnight blue triangles and was gone.

As her soliloquy went on, she seemed entranced by the journey of her imagination, oblivious to my presence. Until she stopped abruptly.

"I was just about to ask the dragonfly about Mrs. Tiggy-Winkle, but then you were waking me up, James!"

By this time, my young self had become skeptical of Sarah's hedgehog fixations. I was in school by then and, to my mind, she was talking baby stuff.

"A dragonfly wouldn't know anything about a story-book hedgehog!" I shouted. "How can you be so silly?"

"It was a dream, a dream! Oh what do... what do you know," she said, getting up and marching off, leaving her pole leaning against the fence.

That night I could faintly hear Sarah on her pennywhistle, playing something that I couldn't make out. It wasn't a tune at all, just a repeated pattern, always starting low and stepping up, but with a rhythm to it that tugged at some string of a memory. It was something like a dance, I think, but played slowly. It went on and on until it wasn't pleasing at all ... more like an itch I couldn't scratch. She finally played another pattern—much like the first but starting high and then moving lower—somehow scratching the itch. And then she stopped.

I looked toward the window, and the shadows on the walls of my room deepened around me. I felt my heart throbbing inside my temples.

Sarah's dragonfly dream came back to me. She wouldn't let it go and was just positive that the lake in her dream was a real place—even if she allowed that the dragonfly ride was not. We tried following the stream down to another lake as she had done in her dream. But we came to a place where the stream flowed through a concrete pipe that led under the highway. Looking through the pipe, we saw only blackness. Our way was blocked. But the trip over to the stream's end became one of our regular excursions, a stopping place where we'd stare into the black pipe and wonder about the ponds, meadows, and creatures on the other side.

One afternoon without really thinking about it, we wandered into a clearing not far from the old black pipe. On the other side, we noticed a dirt road. Taking a few steps along it, we suddenly found ourselves looking down onto mounds of dirt and piles of stones filling a small valley. There was a bulldozer there and a man climbing up onto it. We had come upon him suddenly. Startled, he shouted at us and started running at us.

"You kids don't belong here!" he yelled. "What the devil!"

We ran away from him into the woods and could hear his heavy crashing behind us. We tripped over roots as we scurried along but seemed to be getting away at last. We could hear the noise of cars coming near and then above us the embankment of the highway.

We turned to the left, totally lost and out of our element by this time. After a few minutes walking along below the embankment, we stumbled out into an opening for a footpath tunnel under the highway. (I learned much later that this mysterious passageway was created for farmers to cross with their dairy herds, but it had since become a forgotten byway.) We didn't want to go any farther because we were now far from home and getting farther. We thought we'd lost the man who'd been following us and so moved toward the path away from the highway. Suddenly, we heard the trampling of horse's hooves and turned to see a man on horseback now filling the shadows of the tunnel under the highway.

Mr. Stiles himself was right on top of us.

"What are you kids doing way out here?" he barked. "You'll get the dickens when your folks find out I saw you out by the highway!"

Then he slid off his horse and swooped Sarah up and onto the saddle. It happened so quickly I couldn't imagine how he managed to take off so quickly with Sarah seated in front of him. She looked toward me but her hair had tumbled across her face and I couldn't see her eyes.

"You can find your way home, boy, I'll get Sarah back to her dad," Mr. Stiles yelled back at me.

I could only watch them gallop away.

§   §   §

I stopped reading at this point. There was one more short section before the Later Years began, but I needed time to think about the world I had just been part of. The character of Sarah had intrigued me since the beginning. I kept wondering whom she was based on. Maybe she had a bit of me, a bit of his sister, a bit of our daughter when she was a child? But Sarah was actually different from all of us. Was it an old girlfriend, a childhood playmate? Todd never told me about anyone in his life who was like Sarah. She's his own fictional creation, surely, but the inspiration for her must have come from somewhere.

Then I remembered watching a movie with Todd about the life of Beatrix Potter, whose books Sarah loved so well. The young Beatrix is portrayed in the movie as a young girl with a vivid imagination, who was always telling stories to her little brother, her animal characters alive in her mind, her words, and her drawings. Sarah's extended soliloquy about her dream could have been part of that movie if Beatrix had ever written a tale about dragonflies.

That night I watched the movie again. There was surely some of young Beatrix in Sarah, I thought, but with one very important difference. Beatrix had grown up in a wealthy family, where she could indulge her creative passions despite her mother's disapproval. Todd had created an equally imaginative soul in Sarah, who did not enjoy the same privileged upbringing.

The movie included the part of Beatrix's story after she became a successful author. Though in her early 30s and considered past marrying age in the English society of her day, she fell deeply in love with her publisher. They were engaged to marry, but he suddenly fell ill and died. The heartbreak was almost too much for her to bear. To move past her grief, Beatrix resolved to make a dramatic life change. She left her parents' London house where she had lived her whole life and bought an old farm in the Lake District. There she found contentment and inspiration. She created a new identity for herself as the owner of a working farm and a land conservation practitioner while continuing to write and draw. A few years later, she found love again and married.

In a sense, the person Beatrix was before her fiancé's death died along with him. Her new life seemed equally beautiful to the one she might have had with him. Though the movie tells an idealized version of the tale, it led me to wonder if my own search for a new identity could have the same result. Should I sell the house Todd and I had shared, leaving behind the beautiful kitchen cabinets he had built, the garage where he crafted beautiful boats and carved violins, the room where he breathed his last breath? Should I move somewhere that would be mine alone, something that would reflect the new self I aspired to become?

For now, this would remain an open question. Before I could contemplate such a daunting and emotional task, I needed to finish Todd's book here in the house where we had spent our best years as a couple. How long would that take? It was not something I wanted to rush.

A few days later, I was ready to pick up the book again. It resumed several years after the incident that ended with Sarah getting whisked off on a horse by Mr. Stiles.

§   §   §

Cottage at the Cinder Path

Early Years: Chapter 5

Our family's wing had old-fashioned call boxes so that the Stiles could summon a servant to one of their rooms. When it buzzed, a black triangle dropped into the little square representing the indicated room. My dad, who was the handyman as well as the groom, had installed an intercom system to replace the buzzer boxes, but Mr. Stiles insisted that the old black boxes remain as well.

Stiles liked a cognac in his sitting room in the evening, so Mom would wait for the buzzer, look up for the box of the room, and then drop her knitting. It took only a few steps for her to get to the Stiles' sitting room. The servants' wing was a helter-skelter affair that dipped down from the main house by half a story and connected with uneven ramps and flights of stairs from each floor. So Mom would walk slightly downhill along a ramp-like hallway and then turn onto a short flight that ended at a landing just outside a doorway to the sitting room.

One night, the intercom went off just as the flag dropped and Mr. Stiles asked if "the boy can come along tonight."

Mom jumped to her feet and walked over to the intercom to hold down the button.

"Begging your pardon, Mr. Stiles," she said. "I can't see that's a right thing for the boy. I'll be right up myself."

In a few minutes, she was back and had that angry look about her as if I'd done something wrong.

"Well, that isn't gonna happen," she said. "I'd sooner starve than have my boy serve that man his brandy!"

"James is a bit young for that," my dad agreed. "Not at his age, for certain."

"His age ... his age. My God! Not any age for my boy."

I thought of the little exchange for years, every time the Stiles had me into their parlor in the evening. I never did pour brandy in the sitting room, but I soon had a pair of L.L. Bean duck boots and a leather vest Mr. Stiles liked me to wear when I mixed the Canadian whisky, vermouth, and bitters for his evening Manhattans. He said he wanted me to dress like I'd just come in from the hunt. The duck boots were brand new and in my size; the vest was an old thing with antler-tip buttons. At the time, I thought the vest was quite cool and would finger the antler tips as I stood behind the bar.

The parlor was done up as a rustic hunting lodge with a 10-point buck on the wall; dark, rough exposed beams, and a painting of a fox hunt hanging over a fieldstone fireplace, which was half the size of the wall. The Stiles had a pair of wing chairs set up before the fireplace with low tables between them. An elaborate TV and sound system took up a portion of a bookcase wall, otherwise occupied by several sets of encyclopedias and other leather-bound books arranged by height. The couple generally watched the news and read the paper after dinner when they had me in to serve the cocktails.

IV. Todd's Childhood Home

About a week after reading the last section, I took the long drive to Stoneham. I thought about how Todd had described it to me. He grew up there in the 1950s and 60s, when it was transitioning from a working-class town of farmers, fishermen, and factory workers to a place where wealthy urbanites were building large second homes, and bankers, accountants, and editors were settling with their families and commuting daily to New York City. Todd's father, who owned an actuarial firm, was among the newcomers who established residence year-round. Todd hated the class divide in the town between the year-round inhabitants of relatively modest means and the monied set, who rarely hid their condescension towards the home-towners.

An elderly farmer Todd called Uncle Bill lived across the street from his family's home, still keeping a few cows in his barn that Todd loved to visit. Todd told me of spending afternoons wandering alone or with his sister or his friend Joey. They would head to Uncle Bill's farm, then to a nearby nature center with shady woodlands and a pond full of turtles, frogs, and fish. His parents kept a horse and a pony that he and his sister learned to ride. Todd was the one tasked with keeping the stalls clean.

When he was 10 years old or so, Todd's parents agreed to host two Ute boys who lived on an impoverished reservation in Utah for the summer. It was part of a church-sponsored missionary program Todd came to despise for its paternalistic attitude toward Native Americans. But he did appreciate the summer he spent playing with Stuart and Raymond. In a black-and-white photo of the three of them, Todd wears a broad smile on his crewcut-topped face as he stands next to a slightly taller boy with long braids facing forward, and another with a short trim, looking away from the camera.

From time to time, Todd would mention Stuart and Raymond and wonder what had become of them. He once tried to track them down and discovered one had been sent to prison but found no trace of the other.

A couple of years after his summer with Stuart and Raymond, Todd was sent to a private boarding school a few towns away. He stayed two years, then on summer break told his parents he wouldn't go back there and demanded to be sent to the public high school in town. They relented. Many years into our marriage, he told me why he had wanted to leave prep school. It wasn't just because of the elitist attitudes that pervade such places, which I knew he despised. Some of the live-in teachers there were in the habit of taking boys into their rooms at night. Todd did not want to become one of them.

After he graduated Stoneham High, Todd started college in Boston. But soon after, his father had a heart attack and died. Less than two years later, his mother sold her husband's actuarial firm to his partner, then sold the family home, and moved to her childhood vacation home on the New Jersey shore.

She informed Todd that she could no longer afford to pay his tuition. So he left college with an associate's degree, suddenly thrust into adulthood and self-sufficiency. He found work first in a boatyard, living on one of the boats until he could afford an apartment. Thinking back, I realize he might have been homeless had it not been for the generosity of the boatyard owner. I believe it was this experience that nurtured his empathy for others in similar circumstances who weren't so lucky, leading him to his volunteer work years later.

In time, Todd moved from boatyard work to house framing and then became a grocery store butcher. Eventually, he returned to college at the state university, pursuing an undergraduate degree in English. That was when we met.

I was in my senior year, coming off a bad breakup, when Todd and I began talking at a party. The next day we met for coffee. Over dinner at a restaurant a few days later, Todd asked me to marry him. I was flabbergasted, not ready to even consider such a decision so early in our relationship. But we quickly became a couple and began living together. We found our first post-college jobs at different weekly newspapers. After a year of living together, we married in a state park under blooming apple trees in a garden beside a lovely old cottage.

My reverie faded as I drove onto the highway exit for Stoneham. Todd had taken me there once on the way home from a trip some twenty-five years earlier. We passed by his family house and stopped at the nearby nature center for a walk. Could I find the house now? I recalled it was on James Street, a turn off the main road just past the Congregational church.

It was a foggy, humid July day, just a few weeks shy of the two-year anniversary of Todd's death. I drove aimlessly at first, turning off the main road at a stone pillar with a plaque marked "Bishop's Cove" that piqued my curiosity. I discovered a neighborhood of weathered cedar-shingled houses in the style found on Cape Cod, many with trailered boats in their driveways. Most of the streets dead-ended at the cove. A squat yellow building with tennis courts in the back had a sign that read: "These grounds, courts, and buildings are for the use of Bishop's Cove residents and their guests only. No loitering."

I decided it was time to find Todd's family house. James Street had more traffic than I recalled from my earlier visit. But the house was still standing, still partially hidden from the road by a stone wall and tall pines. I headed down the driveway for a better look. It was an amply sized home, with a classic gambrel roof and cut stone exterior that gave way to cedar shingles halfway up. A stone archway crowned the front door, and a large back porch looked out over a grassy field bordered by woodlands. I noticed a horseshoe lying atop the corner post on one of the stone walls and wondered if that might have once been worn by a horse or pony Todd and his sister rode.

Across the street was a sign for Stoneham Acres Farm, which I surmised was the place Todd used to go to visit Uncle Bill's cows. I drove across and followed signs for the farmstand, actually a fully enclosed store offering fresh produce, farm-raised meats, pottery, locally made breads and yogurt, and many other specialty items. I bought four ears of corn, frozen chicken wings, and summer squash. My dinner that night would come from ingredients raised on the same soil that was once part of the territory of Todd's boyhood. The farmhouse, barn, and other outbuildings looked newly refurbished, with fresh yellow paint and straight window and door frames. It didn't look like the kind of place a neighborhood kid could wander around in uninvited anymore, but at least it was still a working farm.

Driving back onto James Street, I couldn't miss the large white mansion next door to the farm, with Romanesque columns standing guard at either side of the front entrance. I guessed it had been there at least as long as Todd's family house, an ostentatious display of wealth he would have seen every time he left his handsome but more understated home.

Across from the big white house was the nature center woodlands, with a sign visible from the road marking one of the trailheads. Despite the decades and the many changes, there was still enough left of the Stoneham that Todd remembered for me to better understand the mix of fondness and disdain he felt for the place.

On the way back to the highway, I drove past an expansive brick building that was once the Stoneham Woolen Mill, where factory workers turned out tailored suits that upper-class ladies would wear to church or country club events. The mill closed sometime in the late 1960s, and after sitting empty for several decades became a crafts market called Woolen Mill Reboot.

After my evocative visit to Todd's hometown landscape, I was ready to resume his novella and move into the post-childhood years.

§   §   §

Cottage at the Cinder Path

Later Years: Chapter 1

It wasn't a long trip from the high perch of the stone window frame of my dorm room at the private school my parents had enrolled me in to a small berth in a gray wooden boat tied up at the end of the dock near the Amtrak bridge. From the foredeck I could even make out the towers of the school. I'd landed a job working at the boatyard and, in return for a bunk, a second job helping the boat owner on weekends.

I walked away from my school as soon as I turned 16 and could legally land a job. I'd finally realized I would need some sort of a plan to make an escape from the place, which I hated. The newspaper had run an ad for seasonal yard workers so I managed to get away on a Friday afternoon to show up and fill out the application. I didn't have a phone number except for the one for the school, and I couldn't use that. I was sure I was out of luck when I turned the application over to the man seated at the desk. He looked at me skeptically. I was dressed for school and certainly didn't look the part of a yard hand.

"Young man, there's no phone number on here so how would we even get ahold of you to call you in for an interview?" he asked, looking up at me.

But before I could answer, I heard the scraping of a chair and a tall man suddenly appeared.

"Why are you applying for a job as a yard worker here when you're such a young pup?" the man asked.

"I got my reasons, sir," was all I could think of to say.

"Reasons, you say, reasons. Well, maybe you do. Even if I can't think what they might be. Maybe you do."

Next thing I knew I was taking out my newly issued Social Security card and being introduced to the yard foreman and told to show up on Monday.

During the week, I'd do basic labor. I'd handle the lines and nail in wooden support blocking while hauling fishing boats out of the river on a marine railway powered by a cranky engine probably salvaged from an old farm tractor. I'd scrape and paint the bottoms of the boats perched on the crossties of the hauling cradle—or sometimes knee deep in water.

I wasn't allowed to operate any of the machinery at the time so I was pretty much serving as a mobile lifting device and a spare pair of hands. Sometimes I'd be wedged inside an engine compartment just to push or pull on a drive shaft or an engine block that needed to be taken out or put back in. Other times I'd spend weeks and weeks readying boats for winter storage. I'd drive tenpenny nails into hard oak beams for the boat cradles. I'd help haul the boats and push them into enormous sheds with doors like aircraft hangars.

It was a stroke of luck that found me the bunk, and that made the job work. I'd had no place to stay on the Monday I first showed up, so I'd left my suitcase in the small coffee room the workers used for breaks. The ten or twelve workers at the yard would pile into the break room and sit on old benches and pieces of ship timbers while drinking awful coffee and eating sandwiches and potato chips.

One of the mechanics quickly got wind of my situation and offered me a berth in his old wooden fishing boat that, though afloat, needed some major repairs, including replacing planking, decking, and the entire deck house structure. But it did have a bunk in the forward hold.

Doc, the mechanic, showed me the accommodations after work that first day. His boat had recently been relaunched after the yard had replaced some of the planking, and there was some fresh gray paint on the hull. The deckhouse, though, was a mass of rotting and separating plywood that was leaning like a house of cards ready to collapse. I needed a place to bed down, but I wasn't sure if I could actually sleep wondering if the thing would sink on me. Doc saw my skepticism.

"It has really solid bones, James. It does," he said.

He picked up a propane gas cylinder that was stacked on the dock, hopped aboard, and slammed it down onto the deck. Then he raised it chest high and slammed it down again.

"Hear that? She's as solid as a rock in her bones," he said. "That's why I bought her. She looks rough enough, but the frames and hull are solid. Strong as ever."

I'm not sure why this demonstration convinced me ... rather than drive me away.

"In any case," Doc said, after replacing the tank, "you're new at all this, so I should probably explain that at the dock here we have only a foot or so of water under the keel at low tide, so she has no place to go really, except a short drop into the muck. You'll be fine, I expect."

So we proceeded down the hatchway. Doc was especially proud of the engine room, where he showed off the all-new six-cylinder Cummins diesel engine he'd just installed.

He went over to this wooden panel with valves and switches and busily turned this and twisted that. He motioned me closer.

"Here's the most important part for you right now," he said. "There is a bilge pump that's controlled from the board here. But before you turn it on, you'll have to open this valve that's right above it. So if there's enough water in here to pump, you open this valve and then flip this labeled bilge pump switch. It's right on the lower corner of the board. You should be able to find these even in the dark. Find the lower corner for the switch, and then the valve is directly above it. Here, put your left hand on the valve and your finger on the switch."

I followed his directions and put my hands on the board.

"Go ahead and slowly turn the valve counterclockwise. Don't worry. There's a check valve in there so the water can't come in through the port, only go out. At least that's what's supposed to happen. Check valves can sometimes let water seep in slowly. That's the main reason for making sure the valve is always closed unless you're actually pumping."

I turned the valve a couple of turns and then flipped the pump on. It sprang to life with a gurgling sound.

"That's the sound of sucking air!" Doc said, shouting over the racket. "Turn it off, turn it off."

I flipped the switch off again.

"When there's water to pump, it don't make near that kind of

racket," he said. "It'll be just the sound of the pump whirring away. So now you know. When the pump starts in with that awful clamoring, it's pulled all the water out and you'd best shut her off. And pumps ain't exactly fond of sucking air, as you might expect."

From the engine room, we moved on to the foc'sle, where there were two bunks and a small galley area. He had a two-burner propane camp stove and a small refrigerator, just big enough to keep milk and eggs and such. Doc said that the head was out of commission and that the facilities and shower at the marina were only a short walk down the dock. For some reason, this part bothered me more than the thought of the boat taking on water and settling into the river mud while I was sleeping. I paused a bit as I took in the uncertainty of convenient access to a hot shower and clean towels.

But Doc was at the end of his brief tour, and it turned out I'd have to invent most of the living arrangements anyway. I don't remember using his galley much at all in my first couple of months there. The tiny counter area generally was piled over with small tools and a random collection of marine hardware and miscellaneous boat parts. I'd have to fend for myself, and after a while I got used to the idea of living off sandwiches and take-out. The marina break room was my kitchen of sorts, where I'd keep loaves of bread, sandwich meat, and cans of soda. The marina showers were actually quite nice and had the benefit of a supply of clean towels that miraculously appeared in neat bundles at the beginning of the week.

You wouldn't think it, but it was the sense of solitude down on the river that appealed to me the most. Except during the height of boating season, the docks were pretty much deserted at night. I would move a folding deck chair onto the bow of the boat that was generally pointed out into the river. From there, I'd hear and feel the pulse of the river flowing under and around me. There's always an essence of motion living on a boat like that. Sometimes the motion is hardly there at all; at other times, the boat surges violently against lines trying to hold it fast.

Closing my eyes in the deck chair, I'd imagine myself the sole occupant of a universe composed of low, lapping waves pushed against the hull by the barest of breezes. There were no other people in my imagined universe, only various vistas I could see in my mind's eye: long stretches of golden hay ready for mowing, meandering streams with muddy frogs perched on the wet rocks, ponds and lakes with dragonflies hovering and dancing in the morning sun. I never worked out where the people were. It just appeared to me that way and it seemed at least as good a universe as the one that still had all the people in it.

More often than not, I'd doze off into this reverie and awake with a chill on the deck of the boat. I'd get up and climb down the companionway and make my way past the galley clutter onto the fo'csle berth. The slow, gentle rocking of the river would ease me off to sleep.

I'd often wake up again after some version of a recurring dream I'd been having. I was being chased by an unseen monster and finding myself pursued in the endless maze of a darkened attic. I'd awake each time in fresh terror; relieved that I was not in the attic anymore but in a boat with my ear only inches away from the gentle waves caressing the side of the boat.

The only person who intruded on my unpeopled imagined universe was Sarah. She would be with me in my recurring dream and sometimes at the side of the pond gazing at frogs and wondering about the dragonflies. I hadn't maintained any contact with my family because I knew they would drive me back to school if they could. The world at the boat yard was quite a place apart, with all my provisions within a short walk. A grocery nearby had everything except for the clothes I needed. And even those were few, since the yard insisted that all the hands wear the uniforms they are provided while working. I think the uniform was a great help in establishing a kind of invisibility from the outside world.

I'd been hidden away there for months before I felt comfortable enough to venture forth about town. My expenses were very few, so my little earnings had become enough of a pile to allow me to purchase a bicycle and then an old car from a co-worker. The insurance for the car was my first-ever bill, and I had to visit the post office once a month to get a money order to pay it. By then, I had decided it really didn't matter anymore whether anyone knew where I was. I had a home of sorts and could see my way to renting an apartment if Doc pushed on with his boat work, though I had to admit that the restoration job seemed endless.

I was coming back from the post office and headed back to the docks one day when I was brought up short by a voice hailing me from behind.

"James, it's you!"

I spun around and looked at the woman for a moment, unsure what to do. Did I know her? Then the brown eyes looking at me suddenly jolted me into recollection as she moved closer.

"Oh, James," she exclaimed. "My goodness, it is you. How come you're here?"

"Oh, I work near here," I said. "And live there too. I have a berth on a boat and work at the yard there, and I have a car now and was just at the post so I could mail off my insurance payment."

"Oh James," she said again. "Can't get over it. I'm so happy to see you and it's been so long. I thought you were just some random part of another time, and I'd ne'er lay eyes on you again. But here you are still James and stayin' on a boat,

you say. Almost as if you'd never changed or been away. It's like some story, 'cept it's real."

We talked a bit more, but then she had to go, saying she was overdue at her shift. We tried to make plans to see each other, and I asked if we could meet so she could tell me everything about what she'd been doing and what had happened to her.

She looked down at the ground and seemed to consider. Then she pulled out a piece of paper and scribbled something on it. She handed me the slip and said she'd be working the following day from 1:30 to 7:30, and I could stop by during that time.

"But I don't know if I can bother you at work," I said. "Maybe we can meet after your shift."

"Oh, it'll be OK," she said. "You'll see. It's work, but not the kind you're thinking. Talking to the folks that're there, mostly anyways, is what I do since—it's a storefront drop-in place for people. They gave me a .... Well, we'll talk later."

"What people?"

But she was turning to go with a wave of her hand.

"You'll see," she said.

§   §   §

Part II of Todd's book had been the hardest to read so far. Spending time with this young James reminded me of getting to know Todd for the first time again as college students, hearing his stories about the characters he worked with in the boatyard. It was still there now, a couple of towns from where we lived, and now had a popular restaurant where we would go for dinner. He would always recall something from that time—the old dockhand who would disappear for hours and then be found with green-tinted teeth from drinking the crème de menthe liqueur left in one of the big boats, or the night the hurricane came through while he was sleeping on the old fishing boat.

The dialogue between James and Sarah made me long for more conversations with Todd, more time to do the things we loved together. About a year and a half before he became ill, halfway through the COVID pandemic, Todd suggested we buy a small camper so we could travel. At that point, there was no telling how much longer the pandemic would last, and I sensed he was getting cabin fever. He also seemed to be swept up into a *carpe diem* mentality—let's do what we can while we can. So I agreed, putting my reservations aside. Maybe he had a premonition.

We took that camper to every state in New England over the next two summers and autumns, from Cape Cod to coastal Maine, to the Green and White mountains, Lake Champlain, Rangely Lake, the Connecticut coast, the Rhode Island shore and the Berkshire Mountains. Looking back, I'm glad I said yes to the camper and had those wonderful trips with Todd. Being inside that cozy camper must have felt familiar to him, as though he was back in the cabin of that old boat he lived on as a young man. He would prop himself up in the camper bed at night, with just the glow of a small wall sconce for light, and listen for owls in the surrounding woods.

Our next camper adventure was to be at the Grand Canyon, but that would not happen. Todd had visited there as a young man with his sister and her husband, when he was traveling with them to California to help them move there. I wanted my own adventure there with him, and he was eager to fulfill my dream. But the cancer cut that short. He died just five months after his diagnosis. He had a very aggressive type of cancer that was asymptomatic until it reached Stage 4.

After he died, I could hardly stand the sight of that camper in the backyard. It reminded me of all I had lost, all the things I wouldn't get to do with Todd. I decided to sell the camper and put the money towards a trip to the Grand Canyon. Todd would want me to go. I needed to go, though I wasn't sure why.

V. Rediscovering Sarah

A year after Todd's death, I began making plans for my trip. I found a tour company that offered a small-group, guided hiking-focused excursion, and two friends willing to join me. I sent in my down payment and waited out the months before the date came, taking regular long hikes alone and with friends to build my muscles for the challenges of the canyon. Whenever I could, I ventured back into the world of James and Sarah, always aware that it was my story to finish.

§   §   §

Cottage at Cinder Path

Later Years: Chapter 2

The following day, I did find the storefront on Front Street where Sarah worked. It was a tiny building set apart from the others and had the look of a small convenience store, yet it also had an odd section of fancy brickwork rising above its roofline.

Sarah was inside along with what I took to be a high school student working at a counter and sorting through a box of clothes. There were tables with rows of everyday items, such as soap and toothpaste as well as socks and even some disposable ponchos.

"Welcome to our homeless coalition, James!" Sarah called out as I made my way inside.

She was at a desk in front of a computer, and I stood there awkwardly for a moment until she reached out and touched my arm. "Come sit here," she said quietly. "We can talk."

When I was settled in, she began to explain what this place was all about. "This is my home really. We try to have somebody here from nine a.m. to nine p.m. and so lots of times I'll do a couple of shifts or more. We have some basic stuff people always need and are always taking donations of clothing and such. The city won't let us serve food here, but there's a church a few doors away that serves free meals.

"There's an emergency shelter that's open in the cold months when things get really bad, but during the summers we get a lot of people who come in from the woods outside town or from other spots they find to pitch a tent or lay out a sleeping bag. We do have water and boxes of crackers for folks who need them."

She paused to look more closely at me and asked, "But what about you, James? You say you're living on a boat down at the docks. Isn't that kinda tough as winter sets in? What'll you do then? Don't you need a proper place to stay?"

I opened my mouth to say something but her hand quickly hushed me as it touched my lips.

"I'm sorry," she said. "I can't help but worry after the jolt of seeing you. How many years has it been? You look like the same James. It seems like a lifetime ago, and you've come back from across as wide an ocean as we'd cross over in the stories we used to invent."

"Your stories, you mean," I said. "You're the one who was always makin' up stories and playing tunes on the whistle. And I have to think if I've ever even talked to any homeless people. How come you're here? I'm as confused as if I'd just woken' up and we were in the middle of one of your stories. I don't know anything about how you ended up here."

"Oh James…," she sighed, reaching out and taking my hand in hers. "There's so much I'd like to tell you. And I wish I could. But it's been a very long time, and I just can't hurt you."

She bit her lip.

"Why aren't you at school?" she asked. "I … I heard the Stiles were so generous, and you were at the private school, I thought you'd had the best luck of anybody, for sure."

She brought my hand to her face and pressed it against her cheek.

"I thought that something good had happened from it all," she added.

Just then, the door opened and I glanced up to see a man dressed all in black. He wore a clerical collar and a cross on a heavy silver chain.

Sarah quickly stepped over to him, and he bent down to hug her.

"Who's this young man?" he asked. "Don't think we've become acquainted yet. He spoke in a sort of booming way that seemed to put my presence into the category of a nuisance that could be quickly forgotten.

"James," I said.

"Come on, Sarah," he said. "We need to get the word out. We have to get everybody out for a march on City Hall as soon as we can. Tomorrow, if we move fast enough. The others will be along in a minute with some coffee. We'll have a long night ahead of us of deciding on how to go about it and then calling folks."

Sarah turned to me. "This is Father Russ, James," she said. I nodded and held out my hand.

"Pleasure to meet you, young man," he said curtly.

"Sorry, James! Not the best night for catching up, after all," Sarah said in my ear as she turned to walk off with Father Russ.

This unexpected turn left me suddenly standing by the door as Sarah and the priest walked away.

I found myself back at the boat soon afterward. The river swept quickly by at mid-tide, leaving dancing eddies in the lee of the pilings lining the channel. Doc's boat was one of only a few left at the marina since we'd been hauling out most of the summer boats as winter approached. That allowed me to gaze at the streak of moonlight atop the surging current. A piece of wooden flotsam bobbed on by, likely dislodged from one of the upstream hulks of abandoned wrecks.

Coming upon Sarah after all this time raised confusing memories that arrived in a rush out of the swirling past. I never reckoned to see her again. She and old Tainter seemed to have vanished shortly before I moved away to boarding school. The first summer back, a new gardener was tending the orchards and lawns of the Stiles estate. When I asked after her, I got almost nothing.

"Found a better post, I suspect," said my father.

"Is it close by?" I'd asked. "Do you know where they are? Is Sarah at school in town?"

"Well they was here and then they wasn't. Kinda queer like," he'd said.

"But they had to move stuff out. They couldn't just vanish. Was there a moving truck? Didn't you ask them where they were going?"

"No, they were just gone. Place was empty for a few weeks and then the new gardener started in," he said. "Can't say

about the furniture and whatnot. Could've been they sent for it or … I just don't know. Never did see no truck. but that doesn't mean much since I'm not watching the place."

When I asked Laurie what was up with Sarah and her dad she gave me one of her frozen rope stares.

"Who knows what old Tainter's up to," she said. "Some kinda trouble or another, I'd guess."

"But what? He's just a gardener. How could he be in trouble? How do you mean?"

I wandered about in a daze most of that summer. Seasick-like feelings plagued me over and over as I stopped by our hiding places and walked the old trails. I opened the doorway into the hillside tool closet where we'd pushed and prodded for intimations of magic. Now the dirt just sheltered black beetles that scurried about.

Sarah had been part of me as long as I could remember. We'd been so close it was at times hard to know where my skin left off and hers began, even literally, since we'd so often been thrown in the basement tub together after coming inside covered in mud. Scrubbing circles of foam on her back or stomach was as natural as scrubbing myself. Her toes as likely a target as my own. Her freckles lived in a fleshy realm as familiar as the birthmark on the inside of my right thigh.

The changes that unmade that innocence came later; and I mostly figured the essential oneness of our childhood would hold them at bay. I had never connected her with the wayward longings I'd experience from time to time. They seemed destined to land on a collection of girls wholly disdainful of the idea.

These recollections of Sarah as a small child merged painfully into the mystery of her disappearance. Where had she gone? Where was the Sarah that raised her piping melody into the teeming glen, joining the songs of the chattering squirrels and croaking bullfrogs? Maybe I had done something. My head was all messed up and I couldn't make sense of it.

This thought left me staring into the swirling waters, my stomach churning. Maybe I should ask her if it was something I'd done. But how? When? The confusion of her disappearance rushed over me in waves.

A high cloud swept by, dimming the moon-streaked water to a hazy glow. All that time. What had happened and why? The world bounded by water and work now seemed wrong. I reeled as the vivid memories flooded in and merged with the shock and horror of being sent to a place where men shove their penises into boys' rear ends. A place I had needed to escape from before it happened to me. Sarah and I had inhabited a more innocent world that I missed. Her sudden reappearance after almost seven years, and the blank wall of her disappearance, seemed to be poking shards of hot needles under my skin.

It wasn't long before I saw her again, but in a way I could never have foreseen.

Cottage at the Cinder Path
Later Years: Chapter 3

On my way into town the following day, I ran across a small crowd on the steps of the City Hall. Father Russ was giving an angry speech, and I realized that there was some move afoot to fight the city's decision to close the homeless shelter.

"People have to start to get it," he was saying. "These are not isolated facts. This is evil in the worst kind of way. We have to get people out in the streets to stop this before it's too late, and we all end up in the same place. We have to raise our voices in protest. We have to resist. Demolishing houses, closing shelters, retrieving bodies from the streets. See folks, this is the worst kind of pattern."

Father Russ had a way of stabbing the air with his finger at eye level to punctuate his words. He started to speak faster and to sputter out his message.

"We're headed toward fascism in this country, and our city has a part in all this. This is a fascist policy, and we're just burying our heads in the sand if we can't see it. There's no difference between what our country and city are doing and what the Nazis perpetrated. People are dying. Right here."

Father Russ went on like that for quite a while. When he finally stopped, he turned and motioned a young woman toward the microphone. Sarah. She came forward quickly and looked calmly at the crowd for a moment before speaking. Her red cheeks were set against pale skin in the chill air.

"I have been homeless off and on, and the shelter has helped me out," she said. "They are good people there."

She looked down.

"I know I have made some mistakes, and I can do better on that," she continued. "Lots of people do things that aren't perfect and cost them a good deal of trouble. I'm just trying to make my way. Not having a shelter for folks like me who need it when things are tough doesn't make any sense, especially given the small amount it costs the city to keep it going— a city that spends millions on streets and schools and so many other things. So please help us by signing the petition to keep funding for the shelter in place. People have got to have some place to get to when it's cold and miserable out."

She stepped away from the microphone.

After the rally, I rushed after Sarah as she headed off with her group and Father Russ. But I lost track of her in the confusion. I don't know. Maybe she ducked into a car.

That last passage reminded me how Todd first became involved in the homeless shelter in our small city, New Carlisle. He had become friendly with a local Episcopal priest, Father Ernest Gregory, a balding, bearded Louisiana native who with his wife had started what they called an intentional community. They shared an old Victorian house downtown with several kindred spirits to live the lives of activists, and Todd sometimes joined them in demonstrations calling for government action on climate change and other issues.

When Father Ernest got wind of the city's plan to close the homeless shelter, it had been operating for decades in a storefront, and he enlisted Todd and others to help him spearhead the opposition. Municipal budget problems, coupled with growing resentment toward the homeless and the lack of support from surrounding wealthier suburbs, crescendoed into heated public debates.

Before long, another priest–this one with questionable credentials–came on the scene, calling himself Father Ralph. Several inches taller and beefier than Father Ernest, but with a similar balding crest and beard, he set up shop in a small storefront downtown and rallied local homeless people around him with bombastic speeches on the City Hall steps. Some of the homeless started living with him in the storefront.

Father Ralph spurned Ernest's appeals to join forces with him. Todd felt Father Ralph wielded too much power, and couldn't be trusted.

The rest of the story is a blur. A new shelter opened up, a nonprofit run by Father Ernest. Todd and others helped start it, with money from grants and donations. Father Ralph disappeared from the scene. Todd started volunteering regularly at this shelter, and sometimes I would go to help him serve sandwiches. Once, as I handed a tuna on wheat bread to a middle-aged man, he thanked me and began telling me his story. He had been a teacher, but then his wife left him suddenly and drained their bank accounts. He fell into debt, lost his job, and was evicted from his apartment. I was a total stranger to him, yet I think he recovered a bit of his dignity by sharing his story spontaneously with me–at least I hope so. I could no longer look upon him as just "homeless," but as a dignified individual with a unique story.

VI: Nature's Healing Ways

I am ashamed to admit that, at one point, I wanted Todd to stop his involvement with the shelter. My motives were purely selfish. At its height, the crisis over whether there would or wouldn't be a shelter seemed to take over his life, and I felt left out. I thought maybe I was losing him. Or maybe I just needed him more than ever then. Our daughter had just gone away to college, and I was missing her, feeling obsolete. I thought maybe he would reassure me if I told him about my fears.

"Todd, can we go for a hike tomorrow at the Jansen Preserve?" I asked him. "I haven't seen much of you lately." "Sure," he said. "I have a shelter committee meeting in the morning, but we can go after that."

The Jansen Preserve was one of our favorite spots, just a 20-minute drive from home, with a main trail that travels from an expansive salt marsh overlooking Long Island Sound to a wildflower meadow and then into a forest with stone walls, an old cemetery, and old foundations recalling the farmers who once tilled the ground there.

We walked slowly across the trail through the marsh, stopping to watch a great egret land in one of the channels and then a flock of glossy ibises beat their shiny black wings to rise from the lime-green grass into the sky. As the trail rose into the meadow, I spotted a great blue heron swaying its sleek frame of marbled feathers as it lifted its spindly legs across the tall grass. It had an intense presence as it moved so gingerly, its gaze fixed on something ahead. Without saying a word, Todd and I stopped to watch. There was a kind of primal energy in the air that we both felt. We waited.

In a flash the heron struck its sharp beak into the grass and stood upright, tightly pinching a long, wriggling snake. It clenched tighter, then swallowed the snake in two gulps. The outline of the snake bulged inside the bird's long neck as it slid down.

"Wow," I whispered. "That was amazing."

"What a thing to see," Todd said softly.

Suddenly my worries felt too small to bring up at such a moment. We had just witnessed the great dance of life and death, hunter and prey, the brutal elegance of wild creatures. Our bond felt as strong as ever.

"I'm so grateful we saw that together," I said. "I've missed you lately."

"I know I've been spending a lot of time with the shelter stuff," he said. "It won't be like this forever."

"I know."

Thinking back on that time, with Todd gone now and the homeless shelter a key element in his fictional story, I felt regret at the misgivings I'd once had about his giving too much time to such a place. But I was grateful that at least I didn't do anything to try to stop him. I saw that through his work there, he'd fulfilled a longing to use his gifts to make a tangible difference in our little part of the world. He became more fully himself during that time, and somehow more able to accept the painful things in his past and problems of the larger world that were beyond fixing.

Remembering that time in Jensen Preserve made me want to return there. I hadn't been back since several months before Todd's death, and now, with the two-year anniversary of that day approaching, I felt a need to be in a place we both loved.

The next day, I left home at 6:00 a.m. for the preserve, hoping to avoid the dogwalkers and chatting friends drawn to the place later in the morning. As I followed the main trail across the marsh, I saw ducks and egrets in the pools made by the incoming tide. The marsh grass glowed electric green in the morning sun. Terns swooped in the distance. Even amid this scenery, the characters from Todd's novella were on my mind. I knew I would be spending time with James and Sarah soon after I got home.

Farther along on the trail, a great blue heron swooped overhead and landed a few dozen feet away, just where the marsh and the forest meet. I froze to watch. This time, it high-stepped into the shady forest and disappeared. Continuing into the woods, I took a side trail to see if I could find it. And there it was, prancing with the command of an alpha predator as it combed the forest floor for prey. For 20 minutes or so, I followed at a respectful distance, as noiselessly as I could. The bird was slow, deliberate and laser-focused as it moved. Then it stopped, training its gaze on a spot on the ground that I guessed was a hole for some small creature. Then it thrust its beak downward, lightning-quick, and raised its head holding a squealing chipmunk in its mouth. It hopped a few steps towards the marsh, then flew up, the rodent still screaming as the heron flew away. I could almost hear Todd saying again, "What a thing to see."

But this heron encounter was different. It wasn't about putting my worries in a better perspective, because I had been profoundly changed by witnessing death, losing my soul mate, and realizing I could live with grief and gratitude at the same time, just as nature lives with both the beautiful and the cruel.

Soon after I got home, I picked up Todd's novella again.

§ § §

Cottage at Cinder Path
Later Years: Chapter 4

The next time I saw Sarah was on Doc's boat just after I'd finished work for the day. I had invited her to stop but hadn't seen her for several days so I was a bit surprised when she turned up out of the blue. We had recently stripped and painted the forward space that held the galley and berths, and there was now even a two-burner stove and a larger refrigerator, plus enough counter space to actually prepare a meal.

I was quite proud of the work I'd done and happy to show Sarah around and talk about the details of restoring the boat. We had recently broken down the deck house and leveled everything off so that there was just a hatchway into the below-deck area. From the side of the boat, there was nothing at all projecting above the line of the railing that ran around the deck. I liked the clean lines with no pilot house or deck house structures at all. We had stacked and covered piles of lumber in the yard that later would go into making the rounded pilot house with controls and the ship's wheel. Doc had saved the original wheel, and I had kept it down below on a workbench. I ended up explaining something of the work to Sarah, including my stripping off the dried and broken layers of varnish.

"Doc said the wheel is made out of white oak," I said. "But all I see is this mottled gray color. He says once I get all the varnish off it, I'll need to sand it down until the wood comes white again."

I'd probably still be talking about my newfound boat world if Sarah hadn't yawned and quickly broken me out of my delusion that this held any real interest for her. I opened the watertight door into the galley area, and we ducked through and sat down across from each other on either side of the drop-down table. We talked for an hour or so, mostly about the Stiles place and our ramblings around the countryside.

Sarah began turning up at the boatyard once or twice a week, and of course I started to anticipate her visits—and get teased about them by Doc and the yard hands.

By this time, I'd managed to acquire a small skiff with an outboard that I kept tied up at the end of the dock. (Doc had helped me find and rebuild an old outboard.) That fall Sarah and I started taking it out on the river, resuming some of our ramblings—but by water rather than on foot.

The flat-bottom skiff was small enough to venture into some of the side channels off the main river, so we managed to wind our way into some of the backcountry, along the sunlit pastures, and into the quiet shadows cast by the spreading branches of the overhanging oaks. One day, we came across a section of winding creek with tall grasses that towered ten-to-twelve feet above us. The air above swarmed with small flocks of birds dashing about above our heads. They all banked in unison, flashing and then hiding the red stripes emblazoned on their black wings as they whirled across the sky. A little farther along, we stumbled upon a small, shady beach. I pulled the skiff into the shallows and cut the motor so we could drift onto the sand.

Sarah had packed a lunch, which she handed to me in a paper bag before stepping out of the boat from the bow onto the sand. We scrambled up the rock outcropping that rose off to the side of the beach. From there we had a view of a network of creeks, channels, and small pools glistening among this land of tall grasses we'd just discovered. I wanted to put my arm around Sarah, but hesitated. That was not something we'd ever done.

"What is this place?" Sarah asked as she unpacked the cheese, bread, and bottles of iced tea. "I've never seen anything like it."

From our vantage point, we could make out hundreds, maybe thousands, of redwings darting about the landscape. Since I'd been here a few times, I'd looked for it on a chart at the marina.

"It doesn't seem like a cove because it's mostly all filled up," I told Sarah. "But they call this place Whalebone Cove. I think that they got the name from the rock formation out by

the entrance that has marble running through, like bones. But maybe it takes some imagination though," I admitted.

"I've never seen these towering grasses," Sarah said. "They're way, way over our heads. They almost seem like something from another world. What are they?"

"I took a handful of the stems and seeds back last time I was out here and asked old Wally at the marina about them," I said.

"Oh, you've gone and found Whalebone Cove," Wally told me. "Now don't go tearin' 'round in there! You hear me? That's a special kind of place, and there's nothing else like it anywhere around. That's wild rice sure enough, and it attracts birds by the thousands when it ripens up. Indians 'round here used to harvest it, but now it's best to leave it because there's only this one patch and all."

"The sight of the wild rice seemed to light old Wally up and get him talking like I'd never heard him," I said. "I don't think I'd ever gotten much more than a 'sure 'nuff' out of him before, and now here he was fired up about this wild rice stuff."

"I'm sorry to be rattling on again," I added sheepishly. "I'm catching Wally's excitement about the place."

"Oh no, you're not rattling on at all," Sarah said. "I think this place is wonderful, too! I'm so glad you brought me here. It's a real-life fantasyland like the ones we used to make up

as kids. And I sure can use a place like this to escape into after all the … ."

She broke off, looking away to her left and out over the fields of wild rice.

"Well, let's not think of all that," she said after a moment. "It's so swell of you to bring me out here. I just need to focus on how grand this place is. Thank you!"

So we talked a bit about our old make-believe worlds. How we'd gone on and on about children's book characters and made up stories about where they might have gone.

"How is it we thought they were so real?" she said.

"We'd chase all about sure we'd find some of them in some new hiding place," I said.

We were quiet for a while, looking out over the cove and listening to the shrill redwing calls. Then we ate our simple lunch. We both felt the same thing, I'm sure, that we'd found something special in this small moment. I started to say something, but Sarah hushed me.

After a while she said, "I'm opening and closing my eyes, hoping I can keep seeing the same vast fields of tall grasses and feel safe. I'm hoping we'll never have to go away even though I know we have to. But if I keep closing and opening my eyes, I can always keep this place in me."

I couldn't think of anything to say, so I let the silence go on. I think we both wanted that. Suddenly, a chill wind broke the spell. We saw it was getting late, so we packed up and set off again.

On weekends I started to expect Sarah to appear with a picnic basket whether I'd planned anything or not. I don't even think we talked much about planning these trips. They just seemed a natural extension of our previous life together. Even though that was so many years ago, the ramblings seemed to be a logical way to connect, maybe the only way we could be comfortable together. In between there were occasional lunches with pizza downtown. I think I did most of the talking at those times, though. She said she couldn't talk about her work because of the city and the way it treated homeless people as pariahs. Father Russ had told her not to talk about their work in public because people might overhear and find something to use against their cause.

"Father Russ says most everybody in town wants to use the homeless as scapegoats to distract people from the way the city is screwing everybody over," she once said to me in a half-whisper just inches from my ear. "They say the only people making any money are the lawyers for the chain of drug dealers cycling back and forth from the prison to the city."

Her heated words set me back, and I guessed it was best to ramble on about my own work-a-day hewing and chopping. I was sure my life must be painfully boring to someone like Sarah, who was so passionate about her own work. Still, I would tell her about Doc's latest boat project or explain the ins and outs of driving a new propeller shaft through the bottom of a boat. It was such a different world, and she managed to stay interested enough to make it through a lunch together.

"It's a what kind of box?" she said at one point, amused by the marine terminology.

"A stuffing box."

"That's what I thought you'd said. But why? What's stuffing got to do with it? Is there a place for giblets as well?"

"Not sure why it's called that. It's just a kind of buffer thing in the bottom of the boat. Looks like a box and fits around the shaft, and then the shaft turns inside it without letting the water through. Maybe they stuff it with a compound, but no, I'm just making that up. Guess you have to be there!"

These downtown lunches were a rarity and something we did during spells of bad weather that kept us from our outdoor wanderings.

Over time we became as familiar as we had been as kids, puttering about in my old wooden dinghy. We ended up spending so much time meandering here and there that the fittings and boards of the boat became like old friends with their quirks and moods. She was a bit tippy, so shifting about wasn't advised. Her seams tended to leak a bit, so we carried a sponge and a bucket. But mostly she seemed to fit us well. We could trail our fingers in the water as we poked along; stop and drift until we fetched up in a patch of lily pads; stare dreamily at the waving eelgrass under us; or anchor and doze in a hidden cove with nothing to wake us but a joyous shrill cry or the sudden croaking of bullfrogs. There was comfort in finding places we could return to over and over and regain the closeness we had lost but were happy to rediscover.

One of the places we returned to again and again was a small island with a protected cove so shallow we'd often have to get out and pull the boat over the flats as we plodded barefoot through the mud. It sits near the mouth of the river, in the brackish part that rises and falls with the tides in Long Island Sound. The small beach wasn't much more than a strip connecting a section of marsh grasses to the base of a cliff topped by a stand of oak trees. At one end, overhanging oaks created perpetual shade. The small pool of water edging into that bit of beach attracted more than its share of minnows, hermit crabs, and snails that seemed to enjoy the protected spot as much as we did. Slippery brown shards of sugar kelp, white bunches of Irish moss, and floating pods of bladder wrack swirled about in the gentle wave action of the shallow waters.

In the spring and early summer we'd spot horseshoe crabs swimming there. The primeval creatures among the floating wrack in the darkened waters seemed to emerge from a window onto some ancient sea that had sent them far into the future. The shadowed beach was all of 25 feet long, and its gradual slope held extended shallows that hugged the rocky cliff. At low tide, they became a pathway for us to splash our way nearly to the tip of the island.

At the top of the cliff, there was an understory of blueberries waiting to be picked. The small, sweet berries also huddled near the edge of the cliff and then diminished as we moved farther away. The charms of this little dot of an island, especially the thought of its shady corner on the water, lured us there on beastly hot days.

Our river forays became so frequent that we didn't have to plan them, but they'd get rained out from time to time. The gray-slate expanse of the sky overhead looked just the same from a downtown window as from the yard of the marina. We'd both know. No need to bail out the boat today.

I found myself thinking of us as a pair: as "we" and "us." But not as a couple. We were too close for that, too familiar. Not knowing where one's leg ended and the other's foot began. The two-in-one sense of us held sexuality at bay instead of encouraging it. And as we moved back into the primal closeness we had known earlier, we started to fill in details of the intervening years.

By our second trip to the wild rice cove, some stretches of awkward silence started to creep in among our remarks on the acrobatics of the swooping and darting redwings. There were so many things I wanted to ask her, but I didn't know how to begin. Sarah must have felt my awkwardness because one day, at last, looking at me after we'd settled into comfortable perches on the rock ledge, she began to talk.

"James, James, how come you to be here again? I can see you and I can touch you—there's never any doubt of you. I've never known another soul I could tell these things to, and here you are. After all that's happened I don't know how it is possible that we are here together as if we still were just kids. I am happy when we are together. You know I am. But then ... well it's just that I have to tell you some things that are not at all happy. Every time I see you, I want to just blurt it out, but I haven't been able to yet because I'm afraid it will change everything. I know it will change everything. I can't tell you and I can't not tell you. I'm afraid of tearing up all this happy place, but not telling you eats at me because I do trust you, and it's not just about our time as kids. There's a thing that binds us, and it's not romance ... somehow we got past that ... and it's not being kids."

Sarah stopped and looked away. But then something made her look up and then back at me.

"God help me, I can't live with not telling you," she said. "I have to."

And so she began.

"It all ended so suddenly. I was in a dreamland and then was swooped out of it. I'm sure you remember because it was the last time we saw each other as kids. We had gotten lost and Mr. Stiles found us. He came up on us suddenly at the hidden underpass at the highway. Mr. Stiles grabbed me and swept me up onto his horse and then he just ...he just

rode along, and I was so little and had no idea. And then he ... I have to say it ... he raped me."

The earth moved around me. Sarah was running away. Something woke me from my stunned silence and I ran after her and held her until she stopped crying. It felt like an hour or more. First we were standing then we were crumpled together on the ground. I couldn't think to say anything at all.

Finally, she spoke again.

"After that, I don't know," she said softly. "There's such a deep well of pain; I can't really talk about it. You're the only one I've told and that's because I feel I can trust you like I can trust no one else. You'd not betray me or do me wrong, no matter what.

"I guess it's always seemed like that," she went on. "But when I think about it, it always comes back to how hard you took it when the pony died. I know. Silly thing to be thinking about now. That's the way it goes sometimes. I see you even now sitting with her. You put her head on a pillow, and we knew there was no helping her at that point. But you wouldn't leave her. You just kept on sitting there and stroking the star on her forehead and rubbing her soft chin and her neck. She was breathing kinda rough, and the vet had said she'd not last the night. She didn't move except, every now and then, she'd rub her head against you. I'd seen her do that so many times before. You'd be working in the barn and then walk up to her stall, and she'd greet you with

a little nicker of a sound that seemed to come straight out of her chest, and then rub her head into you so you'd have to brace yourself to avoid being knocked over. I'd never seen anything closer to explaining exactly what love is.

"*I don't think anyone knew you'd spent the whole night with her as she was dying. You'd snuck out the window and climbed down the lattice on the side of the house. You'd done that so many times that I knew you'd been there all night when I came back in the morning and you said, 'She's just gone.'*

"*Anyway, I do always think of how you loved that pony even though it wasn't yours. I always see you there sitting with the pony like that and just know there's a part of you that's unbreakable like no matter what sort of bad things happen. I could curl myself into a ball and think of you and the glow of peace you and she shared. Even now James, after all the hurt, I hang onto that. I'm sure that if we love enough, there's always parts of us that still glow because they've been rubbed by someone or something that loves us.*

"*So yeah, I can't tell another soul, but I can tell you. I'll have to tell it all straight out now.*

"*I know now a lot of things I didn't know then but I have to tell it as I know it now. I can't put parts of what I know into little boxes and then just empty out one without the others. It's too muddled up. It's all wrapped up in the memory of the terror, the terror of being thrown down and then the rough hands pulling at my clothes and then the searing pain cutting into me over and over. And then he stopped. I was covered in filth inside and out. I went to pull at my clothes and there was mud and blood all over me, welts from the horrible scraping, blood oozing out of me and mixing with the mud."*

She stopped.

"I don't know when he left. He was just gone, and I was trying to pull my torn clothes back on. I remember seeing the horse's hoofs, first as a jumbled mess right above me and then moving away. I was terrified he'd come back, so I ran the other way, stumbling and falling as I went.

"I just ran blindly through the woods. I really don't know for how long, I finally fell over a tree trunk and just lay there curled up in a ball. I was in shock—as I now know—and I suddenly felt too drowsy to stand up again. I think I just dropped off. I woke up again shivering. Looking around, I thought a nearby stone wall looked familiar. I got up and walked along the wall for a bit. The land sloped steeply down on one side, and I finally came to a spot where a cart path crossed through an opening. I stumbled my way over to the road that leads to the ruins of the old Sweeney farm.

"I thought maybe I should head that way. You remember that the old cart path crosses the state line at some point, and you end up in a little village that's miles and miles away by the regular roads. Nobody would know me there, but maybe I could get help. But who would help some wretched creature

showin' up on a doorstep with nothin' but ripped clothes an' mud everywhere? What was I supposed to tell people?

"*But I was petrified to go home. How could I go near there? The thought of Mr. Stiles filled me with terror; even worse, the dread of seeing my father's face an' him knowing what'd happened.*

"*No, I couldn't go back home. But could I knock on some stranger's door lookin' like the walkin' dead? All that flashed through my mind and heading to a strange place made less and less sense the more I thought about it.*

"*So I started down the hill back toward the Stiles place, about a half an hour walk, and went past the red fishing camp at the head of the pond by the old mill and the dam. I remember passing the dam and crossing the stream below just at the big field below the Stiles' house. You remember, there's no fence as the stream makes the field border, and you have to cross over on a plank somebody put there. I remember doing that, and then I must have tripped or something and, as I know now, I hit my head on a rock. The next thing I knew I was wakin' up in a hospital bed with no idea where I was or how I'd gotten there except that I had all these horrible thoughts that I wished were a dream. But I knew that wasn't true, and none of it was going to go away no matter how hard I'd tried.*

"*All I had on was one of those hospital gowns and so the first thing I thought about was my clothes. I swung my feet over the side of the bed and stood up to pick up a bundle tied with string that was on the chair. At first, I'd thought they must be some other girl's clothes because none of them were mine. There was a pleated blue skirt, which is something I'd never had, and a neatly folded white shirt with a pocket that had an embroidered blue pony on it. Why was I holding some other girl's pretty things? Then the memory of my torn clothes shot through me once again with that rush of horror.*

"I hope I'm not hurting you too much, James, with all this coming out so fast. But for the longest time, every little thing would swing me back around as if I were still there all muddied and tryin' to beat him away. So I was fearful and ashamed for a long time, and I'm sure stuff went on that I don't recall.

"A nurse came in after a while, an' I was kinda scared of her as I'd never seen the inside of a hospital before. She bustled in with a clipboard and stuck a thermometer in my mouth before I had a say in it.

"'Well, you're awake are you?' she said. 'Bout time. You've given everybody quite a fright, child, getting lost in the woods like that; hitting your head. Doctor will be in now that you're awake. You've slept through a day and a night. He'll want to do some tests to check for a concussion.'

"Some of what happened has come back to me in bits and pieces. Some memories and some memories of memories. Some of them still seem sharp as day; some are only cloudy pictures that I'm wandering in.

"They'd put me down as some sort of lost puppy. When I blurted out to the nurse that I'd been dragged about and raped, it was like I was a crazy person. She said, 'Who'd believe that from a wee thing that comes in here with a knot on her head after wandering around the woods and getting all scraped and muddied up? You're talking about Mr. Stiles, who's so kind to you and brought in these pretty new clothes and, as everyone knows, buzzes in and out of town on a helicopter to get to his office where he runs all those TV stations and newspapers? Do you know who you're talking about? What are you thinking, child?"

"Do you get the picture? I mean after all this time ... that gasp still sticks halfway down my throat every time I think of that nurse. It never goes away.

"But you know me. I couldn't shut up about it. It would have been better for Dad if I had. I told him, of course, and he went to the police. Then we were moving away.

"The moving men came and they put everything in boxes and left with them. At first, we didn't even know where they were taking our things. Dad yelled at them and told them that they had no right and to get out of his house, but then there was a police officer saying we were being evicted. Dad told the officer that there was a legal process and papers for that, and the officer just looked at him, shook a pair of handcuffs in his face, and said he didn't want to have to use them in front of the girl.

"A big black car came by and took us to a row house in Beverly, where they'd taken all our things. Dad had to give up the gardening and start work in the mill there, but I think the whole thing just killed him, because his heart gave out, and he was gone by the fall.

"So, that's the brief version, and it's the first time I've ever told anybody. I just couldn't keep it from you anymore. I'd made up my mind I had to tell you or stop seeing you and for a while I couldn't do either."

I wanted to explode with rage while Sarah was talking. But then she stopped, and I was just looking at her sobbing and biting her finger. Some words started to form, and I felt my lips start to move involuntarily as if I had something to say. The words, if there were any, evaporated into thin air. The small, sobbing girl sat cross-legged and bent over, looking into the sand.

My rage turned into a sensitivity I'd never known. I reached over for her hands and her fist opened slowly to my touch. The small package of fingers and flesh was damp with her tears as I held it between my hands so I rubbed them dry as best I could between mine. I still had nothing to say. I had wandered among the dark clouds of rage only to awake in a world full of grace. Her trust in me had opened up that world.

It seemed an eternity since she'd stopped talking, and I continued to struggle to express in words what I was feeling. Every possible utterance seemed coarse or unfeeling or

The Book of Todd

somehow just wrong. Finally, something settled in me, and I spoke.

"Oh, Sarah the worlds of pain you've suffered. What a horrible, horrible man."

With those words, my rage surged up again.

"I'll go after him," I said. "I don't know how, but he's got to be held accountable. People need to know what a monster he is. He can't just get away with it. I'll find a way, even if it means taking it out on his hide."

"James, no," she pleaded. "No. I've stewed over that for so long, but you'll just get infected by the venom of the man. Oh, my, did I muck it up by telling you?"

I leaned over and hugged her.

"No, of course not," I said. "A secret like that eats away at you if it's not shared."

Our embrace lasted for what seemed like forever, until she broke away.

"I need to get to work," she said.

In silence, we climbed back into the boat and headed for the marina. As she stepped out onto the dock, she checked her watch.

"I think I can still get there on time," she said.

"Do you want me to go with you?" I asked.

"No," she said. "I need to be alone right now. The walk will do me good."

I came back to myself sometime that night as the rising wind from the northeast blew in a strong storm. The boat started to pitch sharply, the lashings bit against the cleats, and the rub rails dashed into the pilings. I'd been through worse storms during my time living on the boat. But the tenor of that night's bashing will forever stand apart as a shrill coda to the day I learned a new kind of pain.

§   §   §

As I completed that painful section of Todd's novella, I remembered something Todd once told me, about a girl he knew who lived down the street from him in Stoneham. I'll call her Debbie. Her parents worked at the estate of a top executive in a New York publishing house, and the family lived in a cottage on the property. Todd got to know the girl in high school, and they dated a few times. Then one day, Debbie suddenly told him her family was moving away in a month, and she had to stop seeing him immediately. She wouldn't say why. Todd felt rejected, hurt, confused.

Several months later, Todd was talking with a friend of Debbie's. He asked whether she'd heard from her, and if she knew why Debbie had cut off their relationship so abruptly.

"It had nothing to do with you, Todd," the friend said. "I was the only one she told what happened—after her parents found out, I mean. That rich man who owns the house where they worked messed with her. She was so ashamed and broken. She said her father had told her it was her fault."

To Todd, that story embodied what he hated about Stoneham. He believed those big estates were cathedrals of hypocrisy, serene and beautiful on the outside but full of ugliness inside, lorded over by men who believed their birthright allowed them to take advantage of the less powerful. Sometimes I thought Todd overgeneralized about the dark side of his hometown, but at other times I thought he was spot-on. Certainly Sarah's story tilted me in that direction.

By this time, my trip to the Grand Canyon was just a week away. I knew that the searing climax to Todd's story would never be far from my thoughts, even as I hoped to experience the adventure of a lifetime. Would that amazing landscape speak to me in some way that would help me come to terms with the horrific trauma Sarah experienced and James's devastation at hearing it? Would it help heal my own trauma from losing Todd far too early?

VII. The Grand View

By the time I boarded the plane for my trip, I was ready to pause my ruminations about the last episode of Todd's book. I wasn't going to read further until I returned and could see it with fresh eyes. I was offering myself the chance to be totally absorbed in the natural world, the here and now and the eternal.

But Todd's spirit did come with me to the Grand Canyon, even if his book stayed back home. As I and my friends Jack and Nina acclimated ourselves to the others in our small tour group—a doctor couple from California, a very fit middle-aged woman from Vancouver, and our guide Blake—I told them all I was a recent widow. It was part of my core identity at that point, a key part of my authentic self. I told them that I most looked forward to hiking the Bright Angel Trail, because that was the hike Todd had done as a young man that was so meaningful to him.

Over the first four days of the trip, the physical demands of the long, steep hikes took most of my attention and energy, though I did choke back tears several times when I missed having Todd with me. But then I felt him pushing me forward, turning my gaze to some astounding, indescribable lookout over the vast layers and rock sculptures ahead. Doubts I had held about whether I had the fortitude for the canyon hikes turned to exhilaration every time I completed a trek. I felt happy to be alive, hardships and all.

Over dinner, Blake told us stories about his tumultuous life. He was the child of a drug dealer and a mother who committed suicide, an ex-Marine who bore the emotional scars of combat in Iraq, a body builder who lived out of his car while traveling the West as a hiking guide. Did I really think I would leave trauma stories behind when I came to the Grand Canyon?

On the final day at the Canyon, we hiked the Bright Angel Trail. I tried to imagine Todd there as a young man, rail-thin with hair down to his shoulders like he'd appeared in an old photo from those years. Suddenly, Nina pointed to a butterfly ahead on the trail. "I think that's Todd," she said, smiling.

After about an hour of descending, the trail hugging the canyon walls, Blake stopped at a switchback and motioned for us to gather around.

"Look diagonally across the canyon," he said, waving his hand in that direction. "You'll see the mirror image of the canyon walls right behind us. The whole space between the two sides is the fault. It's where Earth's crust broke open and the two sides of the canyon separated over a billion years ago. If you look down into the canyon, you can see the long, winding trail that connects the two sides."

I fixed my gaze on the other side of the canyon, which was the same warm ochre color as the wall behind me. It was also artfully chiseled across the top and along the face. But it seemed to lean to one side, its position angled toward a different point on the compass. I pondered that image as we continued down the trail.

Back at my hotel room after the hike, I called Todd's sister, Janie.

"I hiked the Bright Angel Trail today," I told her, tired but still excited.

"That's the trail Todd and I hiked with our friends when we were in our twenties," she said.

"I know," I said, "Todd told me. What do you remember about that trip? Tell me whatever still comes to mind."

"We were driving across country to California," she said. "I was married to Craig then, and he wanted to move there. Todd and a couple of friends came along to help us, and we stopped at the Grand Canyon along the way. We hadn't planned it, and when we got there, we just started hiking down. I think all we had were sleeping bags and some water. When we got to the bottom, we bought some Coors at a little store, and we ate prickly pear. We slept out under the stars that night. It was really beautiful."

"Whenever Todd talked about that trip, I got the sense that it was very meaningful to him," I said. "I wish I had asked him why. Do you know why?"

"I think the Grand Canyon is a spiritual place for a lot of people," Janie said. "I think he just felt like we were in touch with something eternal."

We chatted some more about my trip and said our goodbyes. I stretched out on the bed and picked up the journal I'd been keeping during the trip. As I started writing, I realized the landscape had spoken to me that day, loud and clear. I had seen a physical manifestation of life laid out in the rock. That's what I had gone looking for, and I'd found it: the two canyon walls, not mirror images of each other but offset from each other, with a fault between them. One beautiful side of the canyon was my life with Todd, the other side was the full, meaningful life I could have as his widow. I was still somewhere in the middle, on that trail that connects the two sides.

I described these thoughts to Nina and Jack over dinner that night.

"Sounds like you had an epiphany moment," Nina said.

"Yes, I guess I did," I said. "But I was looking for it."

Back home a couple of days later, I decided to commit the image to paper, using some tissue paper and other supplies left over from an art therapy grief support group I'd been involved in. First, I made the two canyon walls by gluing together strips of bright orange tissue paper on either side of the fresh page of artist paper. In the middle, I drew the reddish brown rocks of the canyon, with a bright yellow trail cutting across it. I put myself on the trail as a small tree, with roots that moved like legs.

After about a week at home, I was ready to dive back into Todd's book. There was just one chapter left to read—not really a full chapter, just five paragraphs and a bit of dialogue. The rest would be up to me.

§   §   §

Cottage at the Cinder Path

Later Years: Chapter 5

I doubt I would have ended up working with Sarah's group if not for that day's revelation. I guess people fall out of worlds and into new ones for various reasons. Some changes occur gradually; other changes come all at once and in a rush. The pain of her words cut into me, and searing heat ran through every fiber of my body. The earth turned inside out under my feet.

I couldn't avenge what had happened to Sarah. She didn't want that, but I could take up her current cause. I soon found myself volunteering for the homeless shelter as if I'd always wanted to be there. I was making lobster-pot sized batches of corn chowder on an old cast iron stove in the kitchen of a downtown stone church. We'd serve the soup in paper bowls that we'd hand out from a pass-through counter in the parish hall. It was mostly single men at that time, with a scattering of women. I was struck by the unfailing graciousness of the people lifting bowls from my hands.

"Thank you kindly, young man."

"Gracias, gracias."

"That's a mighty fine soup you're serving up."

The thank-yous in all registers rang in my ears for hours after each night's session. The kindness of these interactions acted as a kind of salve to my wounded spirit. I'd show up on a Tuesday night to cut carrots, open cans, break apart loaves of bread, and clean off tables. Easy and simple. As natural as breathing.

I didn't tell Sarah I was starting this work, but she learned about it soon enough since she worked in the group's office where my name came up on Tuesday's list.

"James, you could have let me know," she said. "It's not something I thought you'd want to do, but it's great, fine. Good volunteers are not easy to find."

Our boat trips up the river and out of the city continued mostly every week. We'd settled into a comfortable pattern where we'd talk mostly about everyday things and work stuff. Sometimes we'd be surprised by some critter along the way that brought back our shared childhood. One Saturday, a swarm of dragonflies suddenly hung in the air by the thousands. The wings flashing all about us seemed magical as we were enveloped within their sphere of rippling color.

Then, one day, Sarah disappeared. She did not come to the boatyard for more than a week and I hadn't run into her when I went to the shelter to volunteer. I thought maybe she was sick, so I asked one of the other volunteers if he'd seen her lately.

"No," he said. "I haven't seen Sarah in a while. Maybe you should ask one of the staff."

So I found Greg, one of the counselors at the shelter.

"She doesn't work here anymore," he said, flatly. "I can't tell you any more than that."

"Can you get a message to her?" I asked.

"Sorry, I don't know where she's gone," he replied.

I felt like I'd been kicked in the stomach. Losing Sarah for the second time seemed too hard to bear. I thought back to the first time she'd disappeared abruptly. Something awful must have happened again.

A few days later at the shelter, still hoping Sarah would reappear, I overheard some of the guests chatting. I had talked to one of them a bit, a gaunt, bearded man named Steve with a front tooth missing.

"He just skipped town, left the rent unpaid at that storefront he was living in," Steve said to the other. "I never did trust Father Russ."

"Me neither," replied his friend. "Maybe you know Joyce? She's come here sometimes. She told me he tried to have his way with her once."

"Figures," the other said.

I felt rage boiling up inside of me. Again? Was Sarah raped again? Did she leave to escape being raped again? She had never been completely able to get past that first horrible episode. How would she survive another? I wanted to help her, to go after Father Russ, but how? The police wouldn't be any help – there's no victim, nothing but my supposition that a crime was committed or at least attempted.

After several mostly sleepless nights wondering if I should have done more for Sarah while she was with me, I decided that the only thing I could do was wait for her to return on her own. Even though my impulse was to start searching, I wouldn't know where to begin. I would stay at the boatyard and keep volunteering at the shelter. Fate had brought us back together once before. I needed to be where she could find me again. And volunteering at the shelter, I realized, was where I had found a piece of myself. By volunteering there I helped ease the pain of others, and my own at the same time.

Then about a week later, I heard from her. I had been working all morning on replacing some of the rub rails on a sailboat when I went into the breakroom for lunch. The boatyard owner's wife Lizzie came in with an envelope in her hand.

"This arrived for you this morning," she said, handing it to me.

I recognized Sarah's handwriting on the plain white envelope addressed to me in care of the Hatchett's River Marina.

"Thank you," I replied, then tucked the letter in my back pocket to read later.

All afternoon I was preoccupied wondering about the letter's contents as I worked. But I wanted to wait until I was alone in my little berth with no distractions. When I settled on my bunk after work, opened the letter and started to read, I could hear her voice in every word.

"Dearest James," she began. "I'm sorry I had to leave without saying goodbye.

But there was no time. I had been staying with Father Russ and some other folks in that storefront, but then everyone else left because they heard he was going to be evicted and then it was just he and I. He started getting verbally abusive and calling me awful names, and saying he could do whatever he wanted with me and that it was my fault he was being evicted. He started pushing me around and I ran out of there and went to the police and told them what happened.

The police asked if I wanted to file assault charges, and I said yes. They brought in a social worker to talk with me, and I told her my story. She asked if I had anyone to stay with, and so I called the last foster mother I stayed with before I turned 16 and went on my own. She said I could stay with her and she'd help me get back on my feet. She picked me up and took me to her house on the other side of the state. Please don't try to find me. I'll come back to you when I'm ready. Telling you my story of so long ago brought up so much pain that I've never dealt with, but I feel like I had better face it now so I can move on with my life. Your friendship has always been the best part of my life, and you will always be in my heart.

Love, Sarah

§   §   §

VIII. Endings and Beginnings

This was how I thought Todd would want his story to end. The instructions he had given me were brief, no more than, "She just goes away." He was too weak at the time to say more. But putting the pieces of the tale together with the Todd I knew, I wrote an ending that I believe rings true.

A few days later, I decided to print out all the pages and read his story from the beginning. As the grinding sound of the printer lulled me into a daydream, I felt something brush against my hip. It was a soft touch, like Todd's when he came up behind me. Was my mind playing tricks on me? Or was this something real? No matter. It was a beautiful thing to be reminded of his love.

Before settling down to read, I decided to clean out the drawers of his desk. It was a task I had put off for months, but now that I had finished his novella, I felt ready for this step. There were dozens of business cards, various receipts, to-do lists and a couple of flash drives that stored some photos. I put those aside to look at later. In the back of the top drawer, I found an unsigned anniversary card with a beautiful message, and a carefully folded napkin from Applebee's restaurant with his writing on it. "Todd is still giving me gifts," I thought.

I opened the napkin.

"Chambersburg, PA," it said at the top. I remembered he had gone to a woodworking show in Indiana a few years ago, and that he called me from Chambersburg where he'd stopped for the night on his way home.

Below he had written a series of phrases referencing metaphysical concepts about space, time, mass, and energy:

Inflating universe increases total S and (m+e) stays fixed

Fulcrum has own relationships

Relationship changed by combination of forces outside of s/time continuum...

S as giving and S as increasing...

Literal Emersonianism

I smiled. Todd's epiphany, scrawled on a napkin, was a treasure I marveled at, even if I did not fully comprehend it.

The final line said: *Traditional/Indigenous: creating finished planks from felled trees and transporting to coast.*

I surmised that his revelations were about the transforming power of life and creativity, about surrendering to mystery. His own boat building and instrument making were expressions of that power. His poignant story of James and Sarah was another. I took his words as a message of hope and affirmation, and I welcomed the mystery that was to be my future.

Maybe this message was what I'd been looking for since Todd's death. My new life would flow naturally out of the one I'd had before if I was willing to embrace the unknown. I could still love Todd and care for him by caring for myself in the way that he and I would want and by opening my heart to others, as he did. I vowed to keep moving along that winding trail to the other side of the canyon, looking back whenever I need to be reminded of the beauty behind me.

Acknowledgements

I want to express great gratitude to all those who supported me through this project with their honesty, generosity, and editing skills, including Lucille Stott, Christine Woodside, Linda Huff, Angela D'Agostino, Judy Preston, Karla Umland, and Ann Schenk. I also want to acknowledge Glenn Cheney of New London Librarium, who generously donated his typesetting and other publishing skills to this project, and Mimi Heldman, who created the most beautiful cover I could have imagined. Special thanks, also, to Richard Telford, Christine Woodside, Lynn Z. Bloom, and Maryam Elahi for their kind words.

www.ingramcontent.com/pod-product-compliance
Lightning Source LLC
Chambersburg PA
CBHW021917120425
24854CB00005B/24